JESSICA BECK
THE DONUT MYSTERIES, BOOK 51
Battered Bluff

Donut Mystery 51 Battered Bluff
Copyright © 2020 by Jessica Beck
All rights reserved
First edition: 2020

The First Time Ever Published!
The 51st Donut Mystery
Battered Bluff
Jessica Beck is the *New York Times* Bestselling Author of the Donut Mysteries, the Cast Iron Cooking Mysteries, the Classic Diner Mysteries, the Ghost Cat Cozy Mysteries, and more.

When Suzanne and Jake accept an invitation from Jake's old friend to visit him at his new lodge on top of a mountain, they figure they may have a chance at a second honeymoon, but once they arrive at Balsam Bluff, they realize privacy is the last thing on the agenda. Not only has their host invited two contentious family members to the house as well, but there are also two disgruntled former business partners who are both out for blood. When the guests start dying, the husband-and-wife sleuthing team must solve the mystery, or die trying.

As always,
To P and E.

Chapter 1

IT WAS SUPPOSED TO be a second honeymoon for my husband, Jake, and me, but in the end, that wasn't what it turned out to be at all. I had recently experienced a close call confronting a killer, and the imminent prospect of my sudden death had made me take stock of my life. The honest truth was that it had shaken me more than I'd even admitted to myself.

Jake—my second and without a single doubt, my last husband, former state police investigator and current criminal consultant—had seen things clearer than I had, and at his urging, I'd left Donut Hearts in my assistant Emma and her mother Sharon's hands. It didn't take a great leap of faith for me to follow my husband to the mountains of North Carolina that I loved so much.

I would have gone anywhere with him.

The only problem was that murder followed us there too, and before we knew it, we were both thrown into the middle of an investigation that nearly cost us our lives.

But I'm getting ahead of myself.

Maybe I should go back and start at the beginning.

"Suzanne, you need to get out of here," Jake told me one brisk morning as he stopped by the donut shop a few minutes before I was set to close for the day. The temperatures were finally starting to drop into more bearable numbers after what had been a long hot summer, and a chill was settling into the air. Though the weather was practically ideal, at least in my opinion, the storm clouds hanging over me were anything but perfect. It had taken me nearly a month before I'd finally felt ready to go back to Donut Hearts after the latest assault, and truth be told, I still wasn't back to my old self yet. I suppose getting shot will do that to a gal; at least it did with me, even if the doctors had described it as 'merely a flesh wound'. There hadn't been anything 'merely' about it as far as I was concerned.

It was my day of the week to work solo at the donut shop, and frankly, it was one that I used to cherish. Lately though, a little of the spark had gone out of it for me, and I found myself feeling more and more ambivalent about starting another day of work at three o'clock in the morning. Honestly, I had to wonder what had taken me so long to feel that way. It was an insane time of night to be waking up and going to work, and I'd been doing it for more years than I cared to think about.

"Give me five more minutes and I'll be finished up here. Where are we going?" I asked him as I started cleaning up a few minutes early. I knew my posted hours were supposed to be until eleven, but there wasn't a soul in sight who looked as though they had to have one of my donuts, so why bother hanging around for a customer who probably wasn't going to show up anyway? Like I said, my attitude wasn't great, but I was too close to the situation to see just how bad it was it at the time.

"I'm not talking about right now," he said sternly. "Well, I am, but not the way you mean."

"Could you make that a *little* clearer? I'm having trouble following your train of thought," I said as I flipped the sign to CLOSED and locked the door just as Max, my ex-husband, raced for the other side.

"Sorry, but we're closed," I said loudly as I pointed to the sign and smiled at him. Over the years, I'd *mostly* forgiven him for cheating on me with Darlene, but there might have still been a *hint* of resentment buried somewhere below the surface. I knew that I should have been able to forgive and forget by now, especially since I'd clearly traded up in the husband department with Jake, but I still felt entitled to a little bit of spite once in a blue moon.

"But it's not eleven yet," he protested through the window as he pointed at his watch.

"True, but it's close enough for me," I said as I turned back to Jake.

"Are you really going to leave him standing out there, begging to come inside?" Jake asked me.

"Would it bother you that much if I did?" I replied.

"Hey, I know better than anyone how badly he blew it with you, but I ended up getting the girl of my dreams, so how can I hold a grudge against him for that?" he asked me.

"Maybe you're just a better person than I am," I said with a shrug.

Jake didn't say another word, but from the way he looked at me, I knew that he wanted me to let it go. "Fine," I said. "But I'm charging him double for whatever he wants."

"I have no problem with that," Jake answered with a smile.

I turned back and unlocked the door just as Max started to walk away. He'd changed on the inside in more ways than I ever could have imagined when we'd been together. He'd married Emily Hargraves, and they had turned out to be a much better match than the two of us had ever been. To top it off, Max had actually done a lot of growing up since we'd split up, and I realized that I really should let the last shred of my anger go once and for all. "What can I do for you, Max?"

"I need your donuts," he said as he studied the case.

There were over four dozen odd assortments of treats left. "Would you like them to go, or are you going to eat them here?"

"They're for my troupe," he said with a grin. Max, when he wasn't off making commercials, fancied himself a stage director. He'd taken an anemic amateur group and had transformed them into a vibrant company by recruiting the only actors around who had the time to devote to his elaborate productions, namely members of our local Senior Center.

"Aren't you worried about pumping those senior citizens full of sugar and empty calories?" It was an odd question for a donutmaker to pose, but I never recommended a steady diet of my offerings to anyone. They were meant to be enjoyed in moderation, not as a steady meal plan, and I was the first one to say so.

"Are you kidding? Some of them claim your donuts are one of the few truly good things they have left in their life. Hey, Jake," he said belatedly. "How's it going?"

"Hello, Max," Jake said as he offered his hand. My ex took it bravely, knowing that Jake could have crushed his fingers in his grip if he so chose, but after a brief shake, they released with no obvious broken bones.

"By any chance do I get a special discount, being that it's the end of the day and these are going for a good cause?" he asked hopefully.

I thought about my threat to charge him twice what they normally cost, but I couldn't bring myself to do it. "I'll tell you what. You can have them all on the house, on one condition."

Max pursed his lips for a moment. "What's the catch? You don't want your mother to star in my production of The Taming of the Shrew, do you?"

I had to choke back my laughter. My mother had never expressed *any* interest in acting as far as I knew. In fact, the only way she qualified for Max's group was by age, though she would be considered an ingénue in this particular cast.

"No, but I'd like your four best seats for opening night, on the house." I figured if Momma and Phillip didn't want to go, I could always ask Grace and Stephen to come with us. They had taken a short three-day honeymoon to Atlanta and had come back to April Springs acting almost as though nothing had changed in their relationship after their impromptu wedding ceremony in our shared hospital room. They were still living apart, though there were plans for that to change soon, but Grace was clearly in no hurry to combine households, and she wasn't even considering changing her last name. She'd been a Gauge all of her life, and she had told her new husband that it was going to stay that way. I'd expected Stephen to balk, but apparently he was just happy that she'd finally agreed to marry him. As far as he was concerned, everything else was just details.

"Sold," Max said with that charming devilish grin of his. "Box 'em up."

"Hang on a second," Jake said as he looked at me. "Suzanne, is one of those tickets for me?"

"That was the idea. Why, don't you want to go?" I was putting him on the spot, and I knew it. My husband wasn't a huge fan of our local productions, but I knew he'd have fun once he was there.

"That's not it. I've just made plans for us for the next four days."

That was news to me. "What are they?"

He glanced at Max. "Let's get him set up first and then we can talk about it," Jake answered. "When is the play set to start?"

"Opening night isn't for a month, so you've got plenty of time," Max said.

"That's a long time to rehearse, isn't it?" Jake asked him.

"I want everything to be perfect," Max answered. "In a month, we should be there."

As the two of them talked, I loaded donuts up into boxes, happy that I wouldn't have to figure out what to do with the extras, and I handed them to Max. As I got the door for him, I said, "Don't forget your promise."

"I won't," he said. "I never forget anything."

"How about our second wedding anniversary, to say nothing of our original vows?" I reminded him. Wow, where had that come from? I regretted my comments as soon as I voiced them. "That was a bit over the top, wasn't it?"

"I truly am sorry, Suzanne, about everything," Max said.

"Forget it. Break a leg," I said, giving him my most sincere smile.

"Thanks," he replied.

After Max was gone and I locked up a second time, I saw that it was three minutes past closing after all. "Okay buster, you can talk while I work. What exactly is going on?"

"I've already worked it out with Emma and Sharon," he said. "I know you haven't been back behind the counter very long, but it's clear that you need some time away from April Springs. I hope you don't mind, but I've accepted an invitation from an old friend of mine in the mountains for a kind of retreat-slash-second honeymoon for us. How does that sound to you?"

I was about to ask for more details about the trip when I noticed his expression. This was clearly not the time to press him or push him about making plans for me without consulting me. "It sounds great. Let me pack, and then we can go. I'm guessing that it starts tonight, right?"

He nodded, clearly surprised by my immediate acceptance. "It does. If everything works out, we can be there in three hours," he answered. "Thanks for doing this, Suzanne."

"I should be the one thanking you, Jake. I know I've been off my game. Just the two of us getting away alone together sounds like a little bit of heaven to me," I said as I started cleaning up at record speed. Suddenly I felt a new burst of enthusiasm that I'd been lacking lately.

"Er, about that," he said.

"We're not going to be alone, are we?"

"From what he told me it's a huge place, and we don't have to spend time with anyone else there if we don't want to. You know what? As I'm saying it to you I realize that it's not going to be something you need right now anyway. Forget I ever said anything. I'll make a call and cancel."

He reached for his phone when I put a hand on his. "I don't mind having other people around as long as you promise me a little quiet time together."

"Are you sure?" he asked.

"Whither thou goest and all that," I answered.

"It's going to do us both a world of good. Just you wait and see."

"I believe you," I said as I finished cleaning the donut shop so I could go home and pack a bag. Maybe Jake was right. Getting away might be just what I needed to get out of the funk I was currently going through.

Then again, if I'd had a crystal ball at that moment showing me the future, I wouldn't have taken one step out of Donut Hearts that day, or maybe even for the rest of my life.

Chapter 2

"TELL ME A LITTLE ABOUT this place, Jake," I said as we headed out of April Springs toward the looming mountains. I'd offered to drive us there in my Jeep, but my husband had insisted on driving us himself in his classic old pickup truck.

"It's supposed to be absolutely amazing. It was recently built on top of a mountain, and evidently no expense was spared."

"I can't wait to see it, but may I ask you something without ruining the surprise?"

"Sure, fire away," he said as he kept his focus on the winding road ahead of us.

"How did we go about getting invited in the first place?"

"The owner of the estate believes he owes me a favor, at least in his mind. Suzanne, long before you and I met, I was going home from duty when I stopped off at a grocery store to pick up some...it doesn't matter what it was. Anyway, I didn't know it, but the owner of the chain was visiting the store that night when someone decided to rob the place. The perp was hopped up on something, and he had a knife to a teenaged girl's throat when I walked in. The owner used my entrance as a distraction and tried to rush the guy. It was a bad idea, and I knew that I had to act quickly if I was going to be able to salvage the situation. The truth is that I didn't give it a second thought. I had a shot, so I took it. I dropped the guy with the knife and the girl was no worse for the wear, though she was shook up emotionally, but what would you expect given the circumstances?"

"And I'm just hearing about this *now*?" I asked him. I knew my husband was personally responsible for putting away quite a few bad guys and saving the day more than once, but it never ceased to amaze me just how good he had been at his job.

"There was nothing to tell, Suzanne. As far as I was concerned it was all ancient history. Anyway, Killian—that's the grocery store chain owner's name—tried to give me a reward at the time, which I refused. We got to be friends until we drifted apart, and I hadn't heard from him for years until he reached out to me a few weeks ago. It turns out that he sold the grocery store chain and decided to build a place in the mountains, some kind of Shangri-la for his daughter and him. The place is nearly finished, and he wanted me to visit. The truth is that I think he wants to meet you as well."

"That doesn't sound so bad, just the three of us," I said. I saw a quick cloud cross Jake's face. "There are more people coming besides us, aren't there?"

"A few," Jake admitted. "From the way he said it, it's just going to be some of his family and friends. Are you still okay with me taking him up on his offer?"

I thought about it and then realized that there really wasn't all that much for me to be upset about. "Are you kidding? I think it's amazing, and we'll be able to have fun as long as we're together. Jake, you were getting something for your wife at the store that night, weren't you?" Jake's first wife, pregnant with their first and only child, had died in a car wreck long before we met. I felt a shared bond with the woman from the first moment I'd heard about her. After all, we had the greatest guy in the world in common, and I was sure I would have liked her.

"Abby was having cravings, so I was constantly popping in and out of grocery stores on my way home from work," he admitted.

"So then this was just before the accident?" I asked him.

He frowned, and I could feel him tighten up beside me. Even after all these years together, it was still something he was reticent to talk about, even with me. "Yes."

I touched his arm lightly. We were driving his new-to-him old truck up the mountain, and I didn't want to distract him too much from the road. After all, the thing didn't have all that much to offer in the way of safety equipment. Not only weren't there any air bags, there wasn't even a shoulder harness attached to my seatbelt. As far as I was concerned, it was one step above tying a rope around my waist, but at least I had the comfort of being surrounded by a great deal of solid steel. Jake's gas mileage may have been in the single digits, but the truck had plenty of power, so there was no danger of not making it there as the inclines grew steeper and steeper.

"I'm sorry," I said.

"Me too, but it wasn't your fault, Suzanne."

I knew that the fact that Jake had been driving when the accident had happened was a constant source of torture for him, and I had realized a long time ago that no matter what the police report said absolving him of any wrongdoing, he would always feel responsible for his late wife's and his unborn child's deaths. "It wasn't yours, either."

"I know that in my head, but my heart refuses to believe it even now," he said softly. I glanced over and saw a tear track down his cheek. Why had I had to pursue it when I knew how raw the emotions were inside him?

At that point I knew that *anything* I said would only make it worse, so I put my hand on his arm and left it there as a reminder that I was there for him, now and forever.

After a few minutes more driving, Jake pointed to a sign saying "Balsam Bluff" that was barely visible off the steep road's incline. "This is the turnoff," he said as he quickly wheeled the truck off the highway onto the gravel.

"Your friend needs to get himself a better sign," I said as Jake had to abruptly brake and pull his truck onto a narrow lane.

"Don't tell me; tell him," Jake said as he focused on the dirt road, if you could call it that. To my amazement, the pitch continued to climb toward the sky, and I could see a few small impromptu streams off to the side of the road where they had started to carve grooves into the mountain. We'd gotten quite a bit of rain lately, and there was more was in the forecast. I hoped the road would eventually get better before we arrived, but those aspirations were dashed as it continued to get more and more treacherous the farther up we went.

After what felt like a hefty chunk of forever, we finally topped the road and came out into a large gravel clearing in front of a real showplace. I would have liked more time to take in the scene, but Jake gunned the truck and headed for the parking area, narrowly skirting what appeared to be a rather dramatic drop off on one side. There were four cars already parked near the front of the brand-new home, and Jake maneuvered his truck expertly to join them.

As we got out and started to grab our bags from behind the seat, an older man sporting silver hair, faded blue jeans, and an old bomber jacket rushed out to greet us.

"Jake Bishop, as I live and breathe. It's been too long," he said as he embraced my husband. Jake let his bag drop and returned the hug, ever so briefly.

"Killian, it's good to see you. You haven't aged a bit."

"When did you start lying, old friend?" Killian asked with a grin before turning to me. I didn't have a frame of reference as to whether he'd gotten older or not, but the man looked exhausted, though he tried to hide it. Then again, it must have been grueling building a home on top of a mountain in the middle of nowhere, not to mention stressful to boot. "You must be Suzanne," he said as he took my hand in his. For a second I suspected that he might kiss it, but he pulled up short at the last second and then released it. "It's an honor to meet you."

"The honor's all mine," I said as I looked around. "I can't say that I care much for your road *or* the sign that marks the turnoff, but this place looks amazing!" I stared openly at the structure, overwhelmed by its architecture. The massive building offered all kinds of competing and contrasting angles with walls of glass, wood, and stone everywhere. I wouldn't have been surprised if it had leapt directly off the pages of *Architectural Digest* onto the mountain.

Killian laughed. "You were right, Jake. She's a straight shooter, all right." Then he turned to me. "The permanent sign has been on order for months, and the gravel trucks couldn't get up the hill after the rains we've been having lately to work on the road. After the construction crews left, I decided to recut the access road. Believe it or not, the pitch was even worse before! That might have been a mistake, but they've promised to put down a layer of gravel as soon as these blasted rains let up. Come on folks, let me take you on a tour of the place."

"It's kind of you to offer, but we don't want to take you away from your other guests," Jake said as Killian tried to wrestle our bags from our hands. He might have been feeling weary, but it was clear that he wasn't going to let that stop him from playing the perfect host. Jake and I insisted, though, so he graciously, and maybe even a bit gratefully, gave in.

"Everyone gathered here is either a family member wanting something from me or a former business associate trying to force me to go back to the grocery business with my tail between my legs. Sadly for them, they are *all* going to be out of luck. I'm done with the grocery business, and I'm finished giving handouts to people who aren't grateful for them." He reached for our bags a second time, but we again pulled them away.

"We're more than happy to get our own bags, Killian. Are you going to try to run this place all by yourself? Surely you have *someone* here to help you," Jake said to him.

"I have two employees coming tomorrow. There was a misunderstanding on when exactly they were supposed to start work, so there's nothing I can do about it. For tonight and tomorrow morning, I'm afraid that we're going to have to make do with my cooking."

"I'd be happy to make dinner myself," I volunteered.

Killian shook his head. "Nonsense. You are here as my guests."

"Well, at least let me be your sous-chef," I said. "I'm a whiz at cutting and chopping."

Killian was about to refuse—I could see it in his quick glance at me—when he shrugged and smiled. "Why not? Having some company in the kitchen again would be nice. My wife and I used to cook together all of the time before she passed away." He turned back to Jake. "You've got yourself a winner here, my friend."

"Don't I know it," Jake said as we walked into the home through the grand entrance. The floor was dark rough-textured fieldstone, the walls were stuccoed a cream color in the few places glass didn't expose the outside world, and the lighting fixtures were all hand-forged iron. What wasn't stone or glass or iron was deeply polished oak and mahogany. "This place is pretty spectacular," I said in awe of what it all must of have cost in time and materials.

"I'm glad you like it. Leandra helped me design it."

"How *is* your daughter, by the way?" Jake asked him.

"She's barely holding on, I'm sorry to say," Killian said, the smile instantly vanishing from his lips. "She wanted to be here to thank you again in person for what you did for us both, but I'm afraid the doctors are insisting that she can't leave the house anymore."

"I'm so sorry. I didn't know," Jake said, his voice faltering.

"We didn't either, until it was nearly too late. Cancer is an insidious thing, my friend. It killed my mother *and* my wife, and now it's got her in its clutches." He paused for a moment, and then he shrugged. "I hate the thought of losing her, but I've had her for more years that I should have, all because of you. I wouldn't be here right now if she hadn't insisted that I come up for a few days to get away from everything. When Leandra makes up her mind that something is going to happen, I've found it best not to fight the tide." He turned to me and added, "Suzanne, did you know you were married to a hero?"

"As a matter of fact, I did, but he just told me about what happened with your daughter on the drive up. I'm so sorry, Killian."

"Thank you," he said, nodding, though clearly without hearing me. The man was obviously lost in his own thoughts for a moment about what had befallen him, but who could blame him?

"So, do I call you Killian?" I asked him almost as an afterthought. "Is that your first name or your last?"

"You know, it's been so long since anyone's called me anything else I swear I don't remember myself," he said with a hint of a smile. "Killian will do just fine."

"Then Killian it is," I said.

The owner led us upstairs to the first landing that housed several rooms, and then he opened a massive mahogany door held in place by forged straps of iron. I saw an engraved plaque on the door announcing that we were staying in the Tree Line room, and it was easy to see where it had gotten its name. Killian used an old-fashioned brass key and put it on the dresser as he walked in.

"Here you are," he said. "This is one of the best rooms in the place."

I tried to take it all in the moment we followed him inside the spacious room, but the truth was that it left me speechless, which for anyone who knew me was a rare thing indeed. The floors were polished quarter-sawn oak, as were all of the furniture pieces except for a luxurious sofa covered in a rich burgundy material and an easy chair beside it that matched. A massive oak table with live edges sat heavily in front of them both, but they weren't the most spectacular features of the room. That had to be the massive bank of windows that showed off an incredible view to the mountainous horizon and the land far below. I stepped closer to the glass to get a better look and saw that the back of the building abruptly dropped precipitously down. "Wow, that would be quite a fall," I said.

"That's why there aren't any balconies on the rooms facing this side of the mountain. I fought the building inspectors on it, but that was one battle I lost. They said we'd never be able to build here at all, but you can see that I won the war. Balsam Bluff will be here long after all of us are gone."

"I can see how the place got its name," I said. On the drive up we'd seen tons of balsam trees mixed among the rest of the woods, and we were certainly poised on a bluff.

"Sometimes the obvious answer happens to be the best one," he said with a shrug.

Killian was about to add something when a man burst into our room without knocking. "Uncle K, I need downstairs."

"Jasper, can't you see that I'm busy?" he rebuffed his nephew. Jasper was a pale, weak looking man with a nearly nonexistent chin and a fading hairline, though I doubted he was much past thirty. There was a sallowness to his complexion that told me he rarely spent much time in the sunshine.

"It's Beatrice. She's threatening to leave again, and this time, I think she means it."

"We'll just see about that," Killian said huffily before turning back to us. "Will you two excuse me?"

"Of course. When do you want to get started on dinner, Chef?" I asked him.

"Give me half an hour and then meet me in the kitchen," he answered as he headed for the door. "Come on, Jasper. By the way, it's customary to knock before you enter someone's room."

"I didn't have time for niceties, Uncle K," Jasper protested.

"There are *always* time for manners, something you would do well to remember," he said, scolding his nephew yet again.

And then they were on their way out, but I could swear that I'd caught a momentary look of hatred in Jasper's eyes toward his uncle when he hadn't realized that anyone was watching him. With family like that, who needed enemies?

"Can you believe this place?" I asked Jake as I walked around the expansive room after the door was shut again. I couldn't keep myself from touching things. It all hardly even seemed real. Was it possible that just that morning I'd gotten up and started my day making donuts as usual, and now I was in a mountain retreat that we could never have afforded? It seemed as though it had been weeks since the day had started, not just a handful of hours.

"It doesn't surprise me one bit," Jake said as he slumped down onto the couch. "I can't believe Leandra's dying, though. Killian's putting on a brave face, but it must be killing him."

I sat beside Jake. "Of course the man's in pain, but he's right about one thing. If it hadn't been for you, he would have lost her a long time ago."

"That's true enough I suppose, but it's clear that he's wrecked about her condition."

"Should we leave, Jake?" I asked him impulsively. "If our presence here is bringing back bad memories for him, we can be home before midnight if we head out right now." I wanted to stay at Balsam Bluff more than I could express, but if it was too much for my husband's friend to take, I'd head home without a single glance back. Where we were really didn't matter. After all, I'd rather live in a tent with Jake than in a palace without him.

"What? No, of course not. Killian obviously needs us here; that much is clear. It sounds as though his family and his business associates aren't offering him much comfort."

"Then we'll just have to do it ourselves," I told him. "In the meantime, we have half an hour until I have to start helping out with dinner. Come on. Let's explore."

"Is there really much more we need to see in this room?" he asked me. "The bathroom's through that door, and I'm sure it's just as spectacular as the rest of the place."

"I'm talking about the rest of the *building* and the property itself. I want to look around outside before it gets too dark," I told him, knowing that this time of year, night came quickly, arriving even faster in the mountains than it did at home. I shuddered slightly before adding, "The truth is that I'm glad we're not making that drive up *or* down the mountain at night. Can you imagine?"

"I don't even want to think about it," he said. "You're right, though. Let's go see what we can see while we still can," he added as he stood and reached out his hand to pull me up.

"I'm right behind you," I said as I took it. I grabbed the key off the dresser where Killian had left it and tucked it into my pocket. This was a heavy, substantial thing made of brass that felt more real to me somehow than a normal key. There was a *TL* engraved on its face, and as I slid it into my pocket I was happy there wasn't a fob attached to it as well.

Otherwise it might not have been able to fit.

Chapter 3

JAKE STARTED DOWN THE stairs when I heard raised voices below us. "Beatrice, you agreed to stay four days, and I'm holding you to it," Killian said calmly. There was a hint of anger in his voice, but somehow he managed to keep it mostly in check.

"I don't care, Uncle K," Beatrice said. Through the handrails, I saw a lovely young woman with long curly chestnut hair cascading down her back. Even though she was clearly unhappy about being there and scowling quite a bit, her looks were undeniably lovely. "You can keep your money."

"If you leave, I'll be forced to do just that," Killian said. "Are you going to be able to manage the rent on that palace of yours in Nashville without my little *gifts*?" He asked it with a hint of malice in his voice, and while I'd just seen the jovial side of the man earlier, there was clearly another side to him, perhaps one that didn't tolerate anyone going against his wishes. I'd seen rich people use their money like clubs before, and I didn't like it, but I reminded myself that I didn't know the circumstances behind their arrangement, so it wasn't my place to judge either one of them.

"Fine, but I'm staying under protest," she said. I couldn't believe it but she actually stamped her foot like a petulant little child, though she was clearly just a few years younger than her brother. So far, I hadn't been all that impressed with the Killian clan I'd met.

"Come on. Let's sneak upstairs while we can," I whispered to Jake as Beatrice started in our direction.

"Most likely there's nothing up there but more rooms," Jake protested.

"Maybe, maybe not, but we'll never know if we don't go see for ourselves," I told him. I truly did want to explore, but more than that, I didn't want to meet Beatrice after her confrontation with our host. If we gave her time to settle down, maybe things would be a little more tranquil later.

It was worth a shot anyway.

"I'm coming, I'm coming," Jake said as I grabbed his hand and pulled him up the stairs. "I just hope her room isn't up there. How are we going to explain our presence then?"

"We're exploring, remember?" I asked him. "That should forgive all sorts of sins."

"I didn't realize you had sinning in mind," he said with a grin as he followed me up the stairs. "Now you've got my attention."

I started to laugh, but then quickly stifled it. We made our way up the stairs and past another floor of rooms.

I kept going.

"*More* steps?"

"Come on, it's a good workout," I chided him. I really did want to see what was at the top now.

"It's probably just Killian's suite," he said, but it wasn't. Instead, the staircase opened up onto a large room that was more of a turret in actuality. There were couches and chairs laid out in a square, all of them facing outward. And why wouldn't they be? From that vantage point you could see amazingly far, even down the so-called road we'd climbed earlier. It was a bird's-eye view in every direction, and as I glanced up, I saw that there was even a clear skylight on top showing nothing but the clouds above us. It was an amazing spot, and I found myself wishing that it was a guestroom, too, and that we'd been lucky enough to land it. That was just plain greedy, though. This way, everyone on the property who was capable of climbing three flights of stairs could enjoy it. I kept going from window to window, taking in the points of the compass and marveling at what I could see. "This is my favorite part of the entire place," I told Jake.

"How can you say that if you haven't seen it all yet?" he asked me with a smile.

"Okay, my favorite so far, then. Come on, let's see what else there is to see."

"Can there really be anything more spectacular than *this*?"

"There's only one way to find out," I said as I took his hand again.

"I'm game if you are," he promised, but as we left the room I found myself glancing back at it one last time. I found myself hoping that a storm would roll in while we were staying there. That scene must be spectacular.

Later I would file that under *BE CAREFUL WHAT YOU WISH FOR*, but I didn't know that at the time.

By the time we got back down to the main level, the place was deserted, though I could hear angry voices coming from an offshoot room tucked away near the fireplace. I tried to hear what the two men were fighting about, whoever they were, but I couldn't make much out other than the fact that their voices were raised.

"Are you actually eavesdropping, Suzanne?" Jake asked softly beside me.

"Me? I wouldn't dream of it. I'm just standing here admiring the fireplace," I lied. It was fifteen feet away from where I was snooping, but the fireplace in question really was stunning. Sheets of hammered copper covered the edges of the enclosure, and there was a stack of firewood ready to be lit inside it. The andirons were shaped in the form of the house itself, clearly having been produced by a real craftsman. A chill was in the air, and I couldn't wait to see a fire lit there so we could enjoy it. In the meantime, though, I couldn't think of another reason to tarry a moment longer. "Let's check out the back porch," I said as we walked to the rear of the structure. The dining room, and what I had to suppose was the kitchen, were off to one side, but a hallway led directly to the back where I'd spotted rocking chairs lined up facing outward.

It was an expansive deck, twelve feet wide with a ten-foot overhang, plenty of room to get out of the rain if needed. The railings were made up of sheets of thick glass with thin metal columns holding them in place, spaced every three feet or so, so no scene was obstructed.

Jake noticed me studying the setup. "It certainly doesn't impede the view at all, does it?" he asked me.

"No, it's perfect. I can't even begin to imagine how much this place must have cost Killian to build," I said.

"Knowing that man, I'm guessing that he didn't let the expense stop him. As long as I've known him, he's never done anything halfway in his life. What's that over there?" Jake asked as he walked toward one end of the decking.

"It's a hidden gate," I said. I looked for a latch and finally found it cleverly tucked away into the wall itself. The steps on the other side went down, and I started to follow them when Jake touched my shoulder lightly.

"Should we really be doing this?" he asked me.

"I don't see why not," I answered.

I heard him laugh behind me, but I was already making my way down the steps to the lower level.

The floor below was without any of the niceties ours upstairs had sported. Where there had been oak up there, here was concrete on the floor. The walls had been painted a nondescript builder's beige, and the plain doors, though they looked solid enough, lacked any wrought iron, and the locks were ordinary. I tried one of the doors, and to my delight, it opened. Stepping inside, I flipped on the light switch and looked at what kind of room it was.

It could have been a chain hotel room in just about any city in the country, though it lacked the ubiquitous artwork most sported. Instead, it offered a photo of the mountain outside as its only real decoration. I wasn't sure if Killian was trying to make up for the lack of windows in the room, but it made me feel a tad bit guilty for the splendor we were enjoying upstairs.

"It's kind of stark, isn't it?" I asked Jake.

"I think it's perfect. What more do you need? There's a bed, a nightstand, a chair, and a closet. There have been times in my life when I would have loved to have something this good. It's got all the comforts of home."

"Well, most of them, anyway. A bathroom would be nice," I said.

"There must be communal ones on the floor," he said. "Suzanne, whoever is going to occupy these rooms is most likely here to work. I think it's nice of Killian to provide lodging at all. As you said earlier, that mountain would be tough to drive in the dark."

"I guess so," I said.

He smiled gently at me. "You have a big heart, my love."

"You do, too. I guess you just see the practical side of things more than I do."

My husband took me in his arms and kissed me soundly, something I never discouraged. After we broke apart, he added, "That's why I love you as much as I do."

"But it's just *one* of the reasons, right?" I asked him with a grin.

"Now you're just fishing, but yes, the reasons are too numerous to name."

"Okay, then. I was just checking."

We left the room and, after peeking our heads into one of the two communal bathrooms, I started back the way we'd come.

Jake didn't follow, though.

"Where are you going?"

"Suzanne, there has to be another way up. After all, Killian can't expect his workers to go upstairs by braving the elements. I'm sure he's going to get plenty of snow up here, and I can't imagine that he didn't plan for it."

The thought of tackling that drive in the snow made me shudder even more. How could it even be plowed? "Do you think he's going to be able come up here year-round?" I asked him.

"I don't see how he can afford not to after how much this place must have cost him," Jake answered.

"The upkeep alone has got to be way out of my reach. At least with my donuts, I've got something coming in to cover my expenses, and it's a rare month I'm not able to come up with a little extra to set aside."

"I believe that most people with money think differently than we do," Jake said as he glanced at his watch. "We'd better be heading up. You're due in the kitchen soon." A moment later, he said, "Here it is."

My husband had found the door to the upstairs floors, and we walked up a set of plain pine steps and came out into a nook on the other end of the fireplace.

Killian was standing there alone, deep in thought, and he was clearly surprised to see us coming out of the servant entrance. "How did you two end up downstairs?" he asked us, clearly puzzled by our sudden appearance and caught a little off guard as well.

Before Jake could answer, I told him, "We went exploring. That room on the third floor is amazing. I could sit there for hours taking in the views."

Killian smiled. "I nearly made it my penthouse, but I decided in the end to keep it for everyone who visits."

"Where *are* your quarters?" Jake asked him.

"I've got a room on the second floor that I've loaned out this week, so for now I'm staying down where you two were just exploring," he said, surprising me. He must have seen the look on my face. "I know, folks expect the owner to have a grand suite, but honestly, it's just a place to sleep as far as I'm concerned. I'm happy enough downstairs this week."

"You don't even have your own bathroom?" I asked him incredulously.

"Well, the room I'm in is pretty modest, but I did allow myself that one luxury. Would you like to see it? Honestly, if you peeked into any of them, they're all pretty much the same except for the fact that mine has a tiny bathroom."

"No, we don't need to do that," I said. It cast a different light on the level of comfort in the quarters we'd seen below. After all, if it was good enough for the owner of the place, no one else had any right to complain. My estimate of Killian went up again, and I wondered just how complex this man really was. He had more facets than I'd expected, and I looked forward to getting to know him better. What better way to do that than to cook side by side? "Are you ready to start making dinner?" I asked him.

"Are you *sure* you want to help out?" he asked me.

"Positive. How many people are we feeding, exactly?"

"There will be eight of us, including us three," he said. "I'll brief you on everyone else as we cook, and you can catch your husband up later." He then turned to Jake. "Can you keep yourself occupied in the meantime?"

"I'm sure I can find *something* to do," he said with a smile. "Unless you need my help, too."

I answered the question before Killian could. "Thanks for offering, but we've got it under control, Jake. Have fun."

"You, too," he said. Jake could make one dish—chili—and I doubted Killian was going to be serving that tonight. Otherwise, my husband was not all that much at home in the kitchen. That was fine by me. Our skills were complementary, which helped our relationship, not hurt it.

"Let's get started then, shall we?" Killian asked me.

"Lead the way," I told him.

Chapter 4

THE KITCHEN, NO SURPRISE, was state of the art. Stainless steel countertops, a high-end gas cooktop and two massive ovens filled the space, and there was enough storage to feed an army for a month. I glanced in the freezer and saw row upon row of every kind of meat imaginable, and the oversized fridge had as much bounty within it as well. "I see the supply truck had no trouble making it up the mountain," I told him with a grin.

"It's amazing what a little incentive bonus can do to motivate people," Killian answered with a smile of his own.

"Are you expecting to spend the rest of your life up here?"

"You never know. I might have gotten a little carried away at that, but most of this will keep."

"So, what's on the menu tonight?" I asked him.

"To be honest with you, I hadn't really planned that far ahead. Is there something in particular you'd like us to make, Suzanne?"

I'd seen some nice ground beef in the cooler. "Would you have any problem with my mother's meat loaf recipe and some sautéed vegetables to go along with it?"

"I haven't had a good meat loaf in years," Killian said with another smile. "Take the lead."

"Excellent," I said as we both grabbed aprons and put them on. "What, there aren't any chef's hats?" I asked.

"Take your pick," he said as he opened another drawer. There were indeed hats, aprons, and pants there, all ready for the real chef I was sure would be taking our place tomorrow.

"I was joking. I'd feel silly wearing one. Besides, I don't feel as though I've got the right to wear it. I'm a decent home cook, but that's a long way from being a chef."

"I'll reserve judgment until I taste your mother's meat loaf. I'll be your assistant, so tell me what to do," Killian said.

"Are you sure you don't mind taking orders from me?"

"Suzanne, it will be a nice change of pace, to be honest with you. Sometimes it gets old being the one in charge all of the time," he said with a hint of wistfulness in his voice.

"I only have a staff of one besides myself, so I can't really relate. It must be exhausting."

"It can be," he said, and then the owner looked at me, expectantly awaiting my orders.

"Why don't you chop a few onions and red bell peppers," I suggested while I raided the spice rack.

"Do you want them finely chopped, rough, or diced?" he asked.

"Someone knows his way around the kitchen better than he claims to," I told him.

He laughed, which was a nice sound. "As I said, my wife loved to cook, and I often helped her out much like this."

"I'll take a fine chop, if you don't mind," I said as I preheated one of the large ovens to three hundred and fifty degrees F. Fortunately I'd made Momma's meatloaf enough times in the past to be able to do it by heart, give or take an ingredient or two. I'd even made it my own over the years, substituting chopped bell peppers for the carrots she liked in hers. From the spice cabinet I grabbed some salt, pepper, and Worcestershire sauce. I was happy to see that they had catsup on hand, as well as bread crumbs. It took me a second to find the eggs in the over-stocked fridge, and when I did, I grabbed four of them. I was doubling the batch, which should provide plenty of food for everyone and make enough for sandwiches later if anyone was still hungry.

"I noticed that you have green beans and asparagus in the veggie bin," I said. "They'll be perfect for the sauté, and we can add some potatoes as a side, too."

"Should I get started on those next?" he asked me.

"No, that can all wait until we've got the meatloaf in the oven," I told him. I found a large mixing bowl and added the ground beef, ground pork, onions, peppers, breadcrumbs, and everything else I'd accumulated, including the eggs, after I'd beaten them first.

"Do you need a spatula to mix that all with?" he asked as I noticed him watching me.

"No, I honestly think my hands do a better job," I said. After washing them and removing my wedding ring, I dove in, mixing everything together thoroughly but not overdoing it.

"I've never seen it done quite that way before," Killian said with a grin.

"Would you like to try your hand at it?" I offered.

"No, but thanks for the offer."

The mix was ready, but I suddenly realized that I hadn't greased any loaf pans yet. It was going to be handy having someone helping me out after all. After I got Killian to do what I needed, I scooped out the mixture and patted half of it firmly in place in each pan. After cleaning my hands thoroughly, I added enough catsup to the tops to add some great flavor during baking and then I slid them into the oven. After pricking the skins of a handful of potatoes with a fork and then rubbing them in olive oil and salt, I placed them on a large cookie sheet and slid them into the oven beside the meat loaf pans.

"That should all be done somewhere between an hour and an hour and a half," I told him as the overhead lights flickered for a few moments before coming back on. "Does that happen often?"

"Too often for my taste," he admitted. "We have some power issues up here, but the electric company has promised to run new lines, and in the meantime I've got two large generators coming. They've been backordered, but hopefully we won't have any major power outages until they get here. It's all part of the joy of building out in the middle of nowhere," he explained. "Should we get started on the vegetables now?"

"There's no rush. Besides, you promised me a rundown on who's here at your place tonight."

"I did indeed," Killian said. "Would you like a glass of wine while we chat?"

"Thanks, but to be honest with you, I have a pretty bad palette for it. It all pretty much tastes the same to me. What I'd really like is cup of tea."

"We can do that, too," he said as made us each a fresh cup of tea. While the mugs were steeping, Killian led me to a bench seat along a window in the chef's office. We sat there and enjoyed the view as we sipped our teas.

"Let's see. Where should I begin?" Killian asked. "Let's start with my family. You've already met my nephew, Jasper. He used to work for me in the grocery business, but he was never really very good at anything. I could deal with that when I had a large group of people working for me, but I knew that once I sold the business I was going to have to set him loose to make his way on his own. He has not flourished, I'm afraid," Killian said sadly.

"And Beatrice?"

"Ah, I'm afraid that my niece's stunning good looks have been her downfall her entire life. Do you know how kids often go through an awkward stage growing up?"

"Know it? I lived it," I said with a hint of laughter. "I was a complete and total mess all through junior high school."

"Beatrice has never experienced that. She was a beautiful baby, a charming toddler, a lovely teen, and is now a breathtaking woman in her late twenties. She's relied on her looks much more than she should have, and unfortunately, because of that she's never really had to grow up."

"And you're supporting both of them?" I asked him gently.

"You heard our squabble, I take it," Killian said with a frown. "I'm sorry about that."

"Every family has its issues from time to time," I told him.

"I promised my sister on her deathbed that I'd take care of her children when she was gone. She was not only family, she was my best friend. I've lost so many people I've loved in this life," he said wistfully, and then he shook himself a bit. "But I've had a great deal of joy with them as well, and that's something I'm thankful for every day."

It was the right attitude to have, but I was sure it must have been tough on him. "I get that."

"Anyway, I've decided that it's time for them both to grow up. There's no doubt in my mind that their selfish behavior killed their mother, at least prematurely, and if I continue to let them feed off of me, it's going to kill me, too. I'm telling them that the free ride is over this weekend, and I can only hope they somehow manage to flourish once they can no longer count on me. No matter what the result though, it's time to cut the cord once and for all."

The prospect clearly troubled him, so I decided to change the subject. "You said some business associates were here as well?"

"Yes, but it's a completely different set of issues there. I should have said former associates. Abel Gray started the grocery business with me forty years ago, but at one point when we were having serious troubles, he suddenly lost his nerve. I bought him out, though I had to mortgage everything I had to do it, and he stayed on as an employee. I managed to turn things around, and Abel would have been a very rich man if he'd just had a little faith in us, in me, but he couldn't do it."

"That must have killed him to stay on with the company," I said.

"It was his choice, and the man was a real asset, at least then."

"I take it he wasn't in favor of you selling the business?" I asked.

"He wanted to have me committed," Killian said with a slight grin.

"And yet he's still here," I said. "That must say something."

"I have a feeling it's more out of a sense of self-preservation than loyalty to me. And then there's Vera Whitehurst. You haven't met her, either. Vera started off as my secretary, but she made her way up in my organization to become a minority partner. I thought she had my back, but now, it turns out that she and Abel are trying to force me into going back into a business I've grown to hate."

"Why do they even have a say in what you do with your life, Killian?" I asked. "You sold the business, right?"

"I did, but there are some rather complicated issues attached to that sale. I'm afraid the attorney I used to sell the business was on Vera and Abel's payroll. If the business makes less than eighty-two percent of its sales we made last year, I'm obligated to buy it back, at a reduced price at least, or I have to take a rather large hit.. It wouldn't surprise me if Abel and Vera have both been sabotaging the grocery chain in order to get their old jobs back, but I'm going to tell them tomorrow that I'd rather eat the penalties involved than to go back into business with them."

"How bad *are* the penalties?"

"It's two million dollars I'd rather not lose, but what is my freedom worth? Certainly more than that," he said. Two million? He was a stronger person than I was. That kind of penalty would be overwhelming for just about most people.

Clearly his former business associates didn't realize that Killian wasn't most people.

"What's your daughter think about the situation?" I asked him.

"She just wants me to be happy," he said. "Besides, she made enough off the sale to live comfortably for a very long time. After my wife died, I endowed Leandra with a seventeen percent share of the business."

"Seventeen. That's an odd number, isn't it?"

"Not when you know the story behind it. She was seventeen when your husband saved her life, and that's been our lucky number ever since. Jake's miracle shot happened on the seventeenth of the month as well."

"Then the anniversary of what happened is tomorrow," I told him.

"It is indeed. We normally have a party to celebrate it every month. As a matter of fact, this will be the first one I've missed since it happened," he said sadly.

"Surely you can get away for it for a few hours," I told him.

"I truly wish that I could, but I'm afraid this time that it's not going to happen," he said brusquely, and I knew better than to pursue it.

I glanced at the clock and said, "We'd better get started on those vegetables. You can help me, or you can set the table for our meal, it's your choice."

"Do you honestly need me in here?" Killian asked.

"I like the company, but no, I've got it covered."

"Then I'll take care of the table settings," he said. As Killian started to leave the kitchen, he hesitated and turned to me. "Suzanne, you're really easy to talk to. You know that, don't you?"

"What can I say? I like to listen," I admitted.

"I know why, too—because you're very good at it," he said. "I'd appreciate it if you'd keep what I told you this evening between us. I'm not used to opening up, and I don't want anyone to know how I really feel about them."

"I'm going to tell Jake, that can't be helped, but we can keep your secrets between us," I answered him honestly. If he'd made the caveat before our conversation I would have ended it then and there. There was nothing, and I mean nothing, that I didn't share with my husband.

"Understood," Killian answered. "I've trusted your husband longer than you've known him."

"Then we're good," I said.

As the rich man left, I noticed that slight stoop in his shoulders again. It was clear to me that Killian, for all of his wealth and power, was nearly alone in the world. If it weren't for his daughter, I didn't see how he'd make it, and from the sound of it, he wasn't going to have her very much longer. Jake and I were going to have to make it a point to be there for him. He deserved to have *someone* in his corner, and it appeared that his remaining family and old business associates were a bust.

As I started putting the vegetables together and getting out a large carbon steel pan, I set about finishing up our meal. It was probably going to fall short of the normal fare Balsam Bluff was going to offer, but I knew that at least it would be good hearty food.

My mother never made anything else.

That just left dessert.

I thought about whipping up some donuts, but I decided to use some pie filling I found and made a nice peach crisp with a crumb topping instead. Once that was in the oven along with everything else, I could get busy on sautéing the veggies. The crisp would be ready along with everything else, and unless I missed my guess, we'd be eating it all in less than half an hour.

My mouth started watering at the prospect of the meal to come, which was always a good sign, at least as far as I was concerned.

I suddenly realized that Killian had told me that we'd have eight people at dinner, but we'd only discussed four of his family members and friends. Besides Jake, Killian, and me, that left us one shy of the final tally, and I wondered who our mysterious eighth guest might be.

I thought about going out to ask Killian about it then, but I had enough on my hands without adding a little snooping into the mix.

Besides, I had a feeling that I'd find out soon enough.

Chapter 5

"WHAT IS *this* supposed to be?" Beatrice asked her uncle as she looked at the meatloaf and sautéed vegetables on the plate in front of her.

"It's dinner, and we're lucky to have Suzanne here to make it for us," Killian answered with more than a hint of frost in his voice.

Beatrice poked at a piece of onion with her fork and then put it down again. "Does the staff *really* need to eat with us? No offense," she added as she turned to me.

"None taken," I said as I gave her my brightest artificial smile. "Sorry if what I made isn't up to your usual standards."

Killian, in an uncharacteristic show of temper, slammed his palm down on the table. "She's my guest, Beatrice, not an employee, but even if she were, that's no excuse for your rudeness."

"Sorry," she said, drawing out the word and dripping it with sarcasm.

"Apologize to her," Killian demanded.

"I thought I just did," she snapped.

"That's not necessary," I interjected. "I've been treated a lot worse than that in my life," I added with a grin as I tried to disarm the tension in the air.

"Perhaps so, but not at my table you won't be," Killian said. "Beatrice, you can say you're sorry, and mean it, or you are excused."

It was clear the beautiful woman was not used to being scolded, and she didn't take it all that well. For a second I thought she was going to get up and leave the table, but her hunger must have gotten the better of her. "I apologize. I'm sure it's...tasty."

"I think it is," I said with a shrug as I took a big bite. I nearly choked on it, but that would have ruined the gesture, so I managed to keep from doing it, though just barely.

"I'll take yours if you don't want it," Jake answered, taking a large bite off his plate as well.

Jasper had a nibble, but then he probably ate everything that way, while Abel and Vera both made modest attempts as well.

Killian took a bite nearly as large as mine, and after he swallowed, he said, "Suzanne, it's even better than it smells, and that's saying something. Are you sure you haven't been classically trained in the kitchen?"

He was just flattering me now, and I knew it, but I smiled at him sincerely for the effort he'd put forth on my behalf. "No, I'm not even trained at donutmaking. I just kind of picked it up."

"You work in a donut shop?" Vera asked, doing her best to feign interest.

"She owns the place. It's called Donut Hearts," Jake said proudly.

"It's a modest little shop, but it suits me," I said. Where had that come from? I loved my donut shop, and I didn't have to justify it to anyone, certainly not the likes of these people.

"I'm sure it does," Abel said before turning to Killian. "You'll have trained staff here tomorrow, is that correct?"

"If they can get up the mountain," Killian answered with a grin.

Did Abel's face go a little white upon hearing that? Vera touched his arm lightly. "He's kidding, Abel. There's nothing to worry about. It's not as though we're all trapped up here together," she said, though it was clear that she had at least a few concerns about the place. Where Abel was tall and slim, sporting a hooknose and oversized eyebrows, Vera was short and a bit overweight. Her roots were in need of a touchup, and her dress was just a tad too tight, but she seemed okay to me.

Sometimes first impressions were dangerous, though.

I was still going to keep my eye on her.

"It's actually quite good," Jasper said, surprising us all after taking another, larger bite this time.

"Don't sound so surprised," Killian said. "Suzanne was gracious enough to step in when our staff didn't show up, and I think she did a wonderful job."

Vera clouded up a bit. "Honestly Killian, I wish you'd get over this desire to get away from the world and go back to doing what you do best. If you were still running the business, you could be eating prime rib every night, not meatloaf."

Our host studied her a moment without speaking, though the silence said volumes. She reddened a bit before he turned to Beatrice, ignoring Vera completely. "It just so happens that I like meatloaf better, Vera. Take a bite, Bee."

It was clearly a pet name for her, and one she didn't like based on the sudden stiffness in her spine. She tasted some nonetheless. Taking the smallest bite I'd ever seen anyone try in my life, she managed to convey the impression that she had to choke it down at that. "Mmmm," was all that she said.

Killian's left eyebrow shot up as he waited, so she took a larger portion on her fork and ate it quickly, as though it was some kind of medicine and not my mother's famous meatloaf recipe.

Did I see her smile for a split second after giving it a fair taste? I couldn't tell—it was that fleeting—but I decided to accept it for what I thought it had been. What did I really care whether she liked it or not? I was pleased with it, and so was Jake. Killian clearly liked it as much as we did, and that was really all that mattered to me.

We were halfway through with our meal when our host turned to Beatrice again. "If you honestly have problems with one of my employees eating with us tonight, I'll warn you now that you're not going to be happy by the time the meal is over."

"I'm sure whoever it will be is fine, just as long as it's not Hank," she said, the distaste clear in her voice.

Killian's grin told me that whoever Hank might be, he was our going to be our eighth and final dinner guest.

A large man with rough clothing and a weathered face walked in, laughing. "Did someone say my name? You know what they say. Speak of the devil and suddenly he appears. Haw haw haw." He bent over the table and took a deep whiff of my meatloaf. "My dear sweet mother's been dead for twenty years, but I could swear that's her meatloaf I'm smelling right now. Tell me I haven't died and gone to heaven."

"Unfortunately, no," Beatrice said softly.

Hank smiled at her and shot his finger gun at her, index finger extended and thumb cocked skyward. "Not yet anyway, Beatrice, not yet."

"Grab a plate, Hank. Suzanne made dinner for us tonight," Killian said with a smile. "How's the road looking?" Before the man could answer, Killian added to the rest of us, "Hank Bannock is my general handyman around here, which doesn't really do him justice. Just know that if someone made it, Hank can fix it, and higher praise I could not give anyone."

"Come on, Boss, you're going to embarrass me," Hank said as he scooped up a massive portion of meatloaf and piled more vegetables on his plate than I would have believed it could hold.

"How about the road?" Killian asked again.

Hank just shrugged. "It's hard to say. A lot of it depends on what happens tonight. If we get some rain, we should be okay."

"And if we get more than some?" Abel interjected.

Hank made a motion of his hand sliding down an incline. "Then she all ends up down the bottom of the highway, but don't worry about it. I think we'll be all right."

"Well, if *you* think so, then I'm sure we'll all be *fine*," Abel said with a frown.

"Worrying about it won't do anyone any good," Vera said as she patted the older man's shoulder.

"Probably not, but that won't keep me from doing it anyway," Abel replied.

Hank finished his first big bite of meatloaf and then said to me, "Ma'am, if you're not already spoken for, I'd like to propose marriage to you based on this meatloaf alone." His grin was infectious, and I was about to answer when Jake beat me to it.

"Sorry, she's taken," he said with a smile.

"Of course she is," Hank answered, doing his best to look crestfallen, though I could see a smile hiding under his lowered head. "Well, if I can't have you as my wife, then I'd at least like to have you as my friend," he said as he offered his hand to me across the table. "With your permission, that is, sir."

Jake laughed heartily. "I don't have anything to do with granting anything," he said. "*She's* the head of the family, not me."

"That's enough from both of you," I said with a grin. "Hank, anyone who likes my cooking that much can be my friend any day of the week."

He nodded. "Now, would it be too much to ask you for your name, my new friend?"

"I'm Suzanne Hart, and this is my husband, Jake Bishop."

"You didn't take his name when you married?" Beatrice asked me pointedly.

"I've been a Hart so long, and I run a business called Donut Hearts, that it just made sense to keep it," I explained. "Bishop's on my checkbook, though."

"You still use a checkbook?" Jasper asked incredulously.

"I do," I said as I shook my head slightly. "I have a landline telephone at my shop, too."

"Seriously?" Jasper asked.

"Seriously," I answered. "I imagine you probably need one up here. I haven't been able to get a signal on my cellphone since we got up on top of the mountain, not even when we were upstairs in the turret."

"Do you mean the tower?" Killian asked with a grin.

"Sorry, tower," I said quickly.

"Don't apologize. I like turret better anyway. From now on it's the turret, not the tower," he declared, and no one was going to dispute it. "You're right about cell service. One of the reasons I built Balsam Bluff was to have a place to get away from it all. What do you think?"

"Honestly?" I asked him.

"Always."

"I think it's brilliant," I replied.

"See?" Killian asked gleefully to his two business associates. "Suzanne gets it, so why don't the two of you understand?"

"Because you can't run the business without cell service," Vera said impatiently.

"I'm not running a business anymore, or did you forget that small fact?" Killian asked her with a smile that held no warmth at all.

"Must we really have this conversation at the dinner table?" Abel asked.

"No, of course not," Killian capitulated. "Sorry."

What was that all about? Evidently the lack of cell service on the mountain had been an ongoing bone of contention between them, but our host had given up the argument so quickly that it had surprised me.

"So, where exactly *is* the landline?" I asked, more out of curiosity than anything else.

"My uncle keeps it locked up in his home office beside the fireplace out there," Beatrice said with a frown. "*We* may be cut off, but he has complete and total access to the outside world."

Killian shrugged it off as he finished his meatloaf and sliced off another piece. I was glad that I'd made a double batch. Regardless of how they'd all started the meal, everyone seemed to be enjoying the main course. "Rank hath its privileges," he said.

"That's why I'm late," Hank said with a laugh. "I was pretty rank before, so I stopped to grab a shower. Haw haw haw." He'd polished off his plate and then looked at me expectantly. "I don't suppose there's any chance we're getting dessert, too, is there?"

"That depends," I said.

"On what?"

"How do you feel about peach crisp?"

"I'm in love with it, as long as the meatloaf doesn't get jealous," he said with a grin.

"Let me clear the dishes and I'll right be back," I said as I stood.

Killian cleared his throat. "You'll do no such thing. You cooked. We'll clean up. Everybody grab your plates and follow me into the kitchen."

"I don't mind," I protested, but Killian took my plate from me as Hank reached for Jake's.

"You heard the boss," Hank said. "You sit right there and we'll serve you."

"Okay, I can see that I'm outnumbered," I replied.

"We'll be back in a jiff," Hank said, and everyone else left the table and headed for the kitchen.

I took that chance to have a word with Jake in private before they returned. "Is it just me, or is there a great deal of tension and animosity at this table tonight?"

"It's not just you," Jake said. "I heard some things while you were cooking that I can't wait to tell you, but I shouldn't do it until we're alone."

I looked around the empty room. "Wouldn't now qualify?"

"You know what I mean. Later," he said as the kitchen doors swung open and Killian appeared with the crisp I'd made earlier. Hank followed close behind with a gallon of vanilla bean ice cream with a scoop.

"Hope you don't mind adding something a little bit extra to the mix," he said.

"You read my mind. I was just thinking ice cream would be perfect," I admitted.

"I'm telling you, we're soul mates, Suzanne," Hank said happily.

The rest of them were all carrying something, even Beatrice, who had a caddy of forks. Jasper lined up the plates while Killian scooped out servings of the still-warm peach crisp. The second they hit the plate Hank topped them with scoops of ice cream, and soon we were all enjoying the treat.

Even if I said so myself, it was delightful, the ideal end to a perfect meal. I was glad that I hadn't let the exchanges at the table between the others interfere with my enjoyment of the food.

"That was absolutely amazing," Killian said as he finished his portion of dessert. "Suzanne, how would you like a full-time position here?"

"I'm honored, but I've already got a job," I told him.

"Well, if you change your mind, there's a place for you. Jake, you can come, too. I could use a head of Security on the mountain."

"Why would he be qualified to do that job?" Abel asked pointedly.

"Jake is a retired state police inspector," I told them. After all, he'd had a chance to brag on me. Now it was my turn. "He was one of the best they ever had."

"Really," Jasper said, and then he bit his lower lip.

"Really," I said.

"What do you do now, Jake?" Vera asked him.

"I'm a consultant for police departments in the area," Jake answered.

"They bring him in whenever they can't solve the case themselves," I added.

"Suzanne," Jake admonished me slightly.

"What? It's true." I stood and gathered our plates before Killian could say a word in protest. "Don't. Say. A. Word," I told him with my sternest look.

He burst out laughing, a reaction the others clearly didn't understand.

"Would anyone like coffee?" I asked.

"Yes, please," Abel said, and there were other nods, all except for Hank. "Can't stand the stuff. Besides, I need to make my rounds," he added. "Suzanne, that was amazing, every last bite of it. I can't wait to see breakfast. You're making us all donuts, right?"

Killian said gruffly, "Hank, she's my guest."

The sheer look of disappointment on his face was more than I could take. "If you can talk your boss into allowing it, I'd be delighted to whip up a batch of donuts for everyone."

"You can dock my pay a week if you let her," Hank said with all seriousness.

"That won't be necessary," Killian said. "Would you mind, Suzanne? I'm beginning to feel guilty about how much work I'm asking you to do."

"I don't mind, and besides, I volunteered, remember? It will be fun," I said.

"I don't see how, but you and your husband are banished from any more duties tonight. Go, enjoy yourselves, while we clean up."

Jake was about to protest when I clearly surprised him by accepting our host's offer. "Agreed."

They were beginning to clear the table again when I pulled Jake out of there.

I couldn't wait to hear what he had learned, and now I'd have the chance to hear everything out of everyone else's earshot.

Chapter 6

"TELL ME WHAT YOU'VE been up to since we split up," I asked Jake as we started up the stairs.

"Let's wait until we get into our room," my husband answered.

"I don't really see any point to waiting, since everybody else that's here is in the kitchen cleaning up."

"I suppose that's fair, but we don't know where Hank is at the moment," Jake answered.

"So if we see him, we'll change the subject," I said. I was going to die of curiosity if I had to wait much longer to hear what Jake had learned.

"Okay. First of all, Vera and Abel do not normally get along at all, but they've decided to work together against Killian in a fairly diabolical way."

"I know. Can you believe it? They're trying to get the grocery store chain to dip below the acceptable level of profits to force him to buy it back."

Jake looked at me oddly. "How could you possibly know that?"

"Killian told me while we were cooking," I said.

"Killian? That man keeps *everything* close to the chest. Why did he just open up to you?"

"He said it was because I was such a good listener."

"Well, he's not wrong there," my husband said with the hint of a smile. "You like him, don't you, Suzanne?"

"I do," I admitted. "He's built an amazing place here under trying circumstances, and he's stood by his daughter's side along the way. The fact that he's lost so many people he was close to in the past makes me sympathize with him. I don't know if I'd have the heart to keep going on like he has, and I admire him for his tenacity."

"Killian's certainly got that. I know the man's not perfect, but I consider him a friend," Jake admitted. "That's not all I found out, though," he added. "If you think his former partners are bad, wait till you hear what his family's up to."

"I'm listening," I said as I grabbed the key and started to open the door.

The only problem was that it wasn't locked to begin with. I knew it had been secured when we'd left—I'd double-checked it—but evidently someone had paid our room a visit without our knowledge or consent.

"Jake, I *know* I locked that door when we left," I said softly. "Did you go back to our room?"

"How could I? I forgot to get another key," he said. "Stay right here."

"Nobody else is up here on the mountain, remember?" I asked.

"Nobody that we *know* of," he insisted as he took out his gun.

"I didn't realize you were armed," I told him.

"Are you kidding? I don't leave home without it anymore," he answered as he nudged the door with his foot and peeked around the corner. As he stepped inside, I was on his heels. Ignoring his command to stay back just made sense to me. After all, I was safer with my husband than I was alone, and even if that weren't true, I wanted to be close to him anyway.

Jake looked around quickly, so I did as well. I immediately saw that our bags had been disturbed, but I knew that it wasn't time to see if anything was missing yet. My husband held a finger to his lips and then made his way to our bathroom. Shoving the door open quickly, he scanned the room before holstering his weapon. "It's all clear," he said.

"I'm not imagining things. That door was locked when we left," I insisted.

"I'm sure that it was," he answered. "Did you notice that our bags were disturbed?"

"I did," I admitted as I went back and looked through mine. "Nothing seems to be missing here, though."

"Mine, either," Jake said as he looked through his own. "I wonder what they were looking for, anyway?"

"Is it possible someone was just being nosy?" I asked as I made things right again.

"If there was any staff up here, I might write it off to a meddlesome maid, but Hank's the only staff member on the mountain with us, and I doubt turndown service is part of his job description."

"I hope not," I said, thinking about the boisterous man possibly being in our room. "Jake, do you think someone else might be here we don't know about?"

"It's a big place, Suzanne," he said with a frown. "I wouldn't be at all surprised."

"If that were true though, why would they be hiding?" I asked him.

"That I don't know, but I've got a feeling it's not going to be good for Killian, no matter what the answer is."

"How much more can that man handle?" I asked my husband.

"You know my philosophy on that. I don't believe we ever get more than we can deal with, even though it seems like it's more than we can imagine at times."

He was speaking from experience, and I knew it, but I wasn't about to say it aloud. "So, what do we do now?"

"We need to have another look around downstairs in the service quarters," Jake answered. "That's the only place we haven't thoroughly checked ourselves."

"We looked at a room and a communal bathroom," I said. "What exactly are we checking the place for?"

"Someone else who isn't supposed to be here, or a sign that they're here, anyway," Jake said. "What do you say? Are you up for another expedition?"

"You know I am," I said. "I just wish I had my softball bat with me." I knew that my husband was armed and more than able to protect us both, but I also realized that I would feel better with some kind of weapon in my hands myself.

"You'll just have to trust me, I guess," Jake said with a slight grin.

"You know that I do."

As we made our way downstairs to the lower level, I asked Jake, "What were you going to tell me about Beatrice and Jasper?"

"It can wait until we've looked around," he said.

"I suppose so," I answered a bit reluctantly.

"Suzanne, if there *is* someone downstairs hiding out, we don't want to alert them to our presence. There will be time to talk about those two later. Let's try to keep our conversation to a minimum until we've finished up down there, okay?"

"Hey, I can be as quiet as the next person," I said as Jake opened the door to the rooms below the main level.

His eyebrows shot up as he looked at me, but he didn't say anything.

I decided to prove my point and not respond, either.

It was the best example I could give him of just how quiet I could be.

And then I tripped over my own two feet and nearly knocked Jake down from behind despite my good intentions.

Maybe stealth wasn't my strong suit after all.

"They're all empty," Jake said after we checked every room in the place.

"I know. That's what's so odd," I told him.

"Why is that?" my husband asked me curiously.

"If the only room we found with things in it belongs to Killian, where does Hank sleep?"

Jake hit his forehead. "I can't believe I missed that. I must be getting too old for this foolishness, Suzanne."

"Don't be so hard on yourself. It was easy to overlook. You were searching for a stowaway, and you had no way of knowing if they were armed or not. I didn't have that kind of pressure on me, so I was free to look around for other things. You can't expect to see everything all of the time."

"The problem is that is exactly what I expect of myself, and you know it," Jake said. "I wonder where Hank's staying? Surely he's not going off the mountain at night and coming back the next morning."

"I have no idea, but I'm surely going to ask him the next chance I get," I said.

I headed for the inside stairs when Jake shook his head. "Let's go up the back way."

"Do you think someone's hiding out there?" I asked him. "It's starting to get cold."

"No, but if anyone's up on the main balcony, we might hear something we shouldn't. It's honestly the best place around to have any expectation of privacy if you don't know about this level down here."

"*That's* the detective I know and love," I said, approving of the idea.

"*Former* detective," Jake reminded me.

"Once a sleuth, always a sleuth," I said, giving him a smile.

"If you say so."

We walked outside quietly, and I heard voices the moment we did.

Evidently Jake had been right. From the sound of it, Killian's niece and nephew were outside talking about something they didn't want anyone else to overhear.

Unfortunately for them, they weren't going to get that particular wish after all.

Chapter 7

"HE'S NOT GOING TO GET away with it!" Beatrice said angrily. I was a little surprised she didn't stamp her foot again for emphasis, but maybe she only did that when she had a bigger audience than just her brother. "That money is rightfully ours."

"Beatrice, he's the one who earned it. I saw how hard the man worked at the grocery. You didn't."

"No need to kiss his toes out here. He can't hear you," she snapped. "Don't try to tell me you don't need the money yourself."

"I may have gotten a bit overextended," Jasper admitted, "but I know when it comes right down to it Uncle Killian won't let anything bad happen to us."

"Wake up and smell the coffee," she said angrily. "He made it pretty clear that he's not giving either one of us another penny while he's alive." She paused a moment, and then repeated, "Not while he's alive."

"Bee!" Jasper exclaimed. "He's family!"

"So are we, but that doesn't seem to matter much to *him* right now, does it?"

Were we hearing the beginnings of a conspiracy to commit murder? I was about to storm up the steps to accuse them of just that when Jake grabbed my arm and held a finger to his lips. I knew he was right—we had to keep quiet and hear the rest of what they had to say—but it was against my nature to stand back and do nothing.

"It doesn't matter. Leandra gets everything if anything happens to him, anyway," Jasper reminded his sister.

"We both know Leandra isn't long for this world," Beatrice said. "All we have to do is to hold off until she's gone, and then it's all ours."

The cold-blooded nature of this woman was chilling the blood in my veins. What kind of monster was she? Beatrice might have been beautiful on the outside, but inside she was rotten through and through, a pretty box that contained only garbage inside.

"You heard him," Jasper said. "He's changing his will tomorrow morning when his attorney comes up here to this monstrosity of a house."

"Then it's not too late," Beatrice said.

"Too late for what?" Jasper asked.

She never had a chance to answer. I heard a door open above us and Vera came out. "What did you two just do?"

"What are you talking about?" Beatrice asked her. "We haven't done a thing."

Yet, I said to myself.

"Stop lying to me. You've clearly upset your uncle. You know what he's been through. Why do you insist on being thorns in the man's side even now?"

"You seem awfully defensive. What's the matter, are you in love with him or something, Vera?" Beatrice asked.

"What? Don't be ridiculous. That's absurd."

Beatrice wouldn't let it go, though. "If it's not true, then why are you blushing?"

"I'm not blushing, I'm angry," she snapped at Killian's niece.

"Lie all you want to yourself," Beatrice said. "I'm getting cold. Are you coming, Jasper?"

"I'm right behind you," her brother said and then, as he walked past her, I heard him mumble, "Sorry," and then they were gone.

Vera stared off into the night and started talking to herself. "What a pair of idiots. They deserve everything they're going to get, which is absolutely nothing."

I thought the show was over, and I headed for the steps when the door opened again.

Abel asked, "What was that all about?"

"Killian finally told them he was cutting them off," she explained. "He said he was using the next few days to take care of all of the problems in his life."

"What exactly does that mean?" Abel asked her.

"I have no idea, but I'm guessing it's not going to be good news for us, either," she answered. "I still think we can turn that around, though."

"You heard him this afternoon before that donutmaker and her cop husband showed up," Abel said. "He's willing to eat a two-million-dollar penalty to keep from running the chain again. If he does that, we're both out of jobs."

"How closely did you read that contract he signed, Abel?" she asked him, clearly pleased with herself about something.

"I saw it just before the final changes were made," he admitted.

"You stopped one draft too soon, then," she answered. "The *last* version had a few important revisions added into the back of it that cost me a year's salary to have included, but it was worth it."

"What did you do?" Abel asked her angrily. "You cut me out, didn't you?"

"Don't worry, I won't discard you completely," she answered with a wicked little laugh. "I'll keep you on in *some* kind of an advisory capacity as long as you keep your nose clean."

"I can't believe you would stab me in the back like that," Abel said as he got closer to her, forcing her next to the railing. We could see part of what was happening through the slats in the decking, and I caught a glimpse of Abel's angry face. The older man looked as though he was ready and willing to kill her in that instant.

"Easy there, sport. You don't want to have another heart attack," Vera said, but it was clear there was an edge of fear in her voice.

"I'm past caring about that," he said. "You've screwed me for the last time, Vera."

I saw his hands grab her shoulders, and the next thing I expected to see was her body tumbling down over the side of the rail and plummeting to the craggy precipice below.

Jake must have seen it, too. Bypassing me, he leapt up the stairs and had the gate open before Abel could follow through and do what was clearly in his heart. "There you two are. We've been looking all over for you," he said with a false humor that was obvious, at least to me.

Jake had wanted to catch them by surprise, and it had clearly worked. By the time I got up there myself, Abel had released his would-be victim's arms and had taken a few steps back from Vera. His face was paler than hers, if that were possible, and I had to wonder if his outburst had shocked him more than it had her.

"I'm going inside," he said as he turned and left without another word to any of us.

"Are you okay?" I asked Vera as I neared her.

"I'm fine. Why wouldn't I be?" She looked at the way we'd just come up. "How long were you two standing down there eavesdropping?"

"We just came outside," I said, lying as sincerely as I could manage. "Why, what did we miss?"

"Nothing. Nothing at all," Vera said as she brushed past us and went inside, too.

"Why didn't she say anything about Abel threatening to kill her just then?" I asked Jake when we were alone out on the cold balcony.

"I don't know, but I've got a hunch we haven't heard the last from those two."

"Those four, you mean," I said, remembering Beatrice's cold plan to kill her uncle before he could write her out of his will.

"Poor Killian," Jake said as I shivered a bit. "Come on, let's get you inside by the fire."

"I've got the chills, but I'm not sure how much of it is because of the cold and how much of it is due to what we just overheard. We need to talk to Killian, and I mean now."

"I know," Jake said. "Let's go find him."

At least we'd be doing something proactive.

That was my hope, at any rate.

"Killian, do you have a second?" Jake asked his old friend as we approached him in his small home office. It wasn't large enough for much more than a modest desk, a file cabinet, and a few chairs, but I saw that there was a window looking out into the living area. I didn't remember seeing any windows on the other side, but I did recall a mirror about where this looked out.

"You installed a one-way mirror?" I asked him.

"What can I say? I like to know what's going on in my home," he said dismissively as though there was nothing wrong with spying on his guests. "What can I do for you?"

"Listen, I don't know if you're aware of the fact or not, but you've got a pair of problems on your hands," Jake said.

"A pair, or four of a kind?" he asked with a forced smile.

I'd been determined to let Jake handle this, but somehow I knew that I wouldn't be able to keep my mouth shut. "This isn't a joking matter. You're not safe here with these people."

Killian saw that I was speaking out of care for him, and his smile vanished. "Suzanne, I appreciate the sentiment, but I've never been the type of man who most folks consider beloved. I've allowed things to go from bad to worse for too long with my family and my former business associates, and I'm afraid I'm finally reaping what I sowed."

"What did you do to any of them that was so bad?" I asked him. "You gave your niece and nephew money and you gave two people great jobs. Are those some kind of crimes I'm not aware of?"

He shrugged. "I clearly didn't think so at the time, but I'm afraid I've been coddling Jasper and Beatrice for so long that they won't be able to stand on their own feet now. As for Vera and Abel, there have been times when they've each failed me, and I've punished them for it. I'm not really proud of much that I've done in my life, with the notable exception of my daughter."

"Then go be with her," I said. "*Forget* all of this. She needs you."

"Suzanne, take it easy," Jake said gently.

"You're right. Killian, I'm sorry. It's none of my business." I hadn't realized how it had sounded until the words were already out of my mouth. Nice, Suzanne. As if this man doesn't have enough reason to feel bad, you just piled more on.

"Don't ever apologize for caring," he said. "I know that you're right, but I'm afraid it's too late. I should have ignored her demands and insisted on staying with her, but that's never been my strong suit when it comes to my daughter."

"I know it's risky driving. That mountain road is treacherous even in the daytime," I told him. "By the way, does Hank commute? We didn't see an occupied room downstairs except for yours."

"My handyman has his own little space, at his own insistence, I might add. There's only one way to access his apartment, and it's from outside. I warned him that when the snow started flying he could get trapped in there, but he doesn't believe me." Killian started to pick the telephone up, but then he put it back down again as he shook his head. "It's too late to call Leandra. I'll touch base with her in the morning," he said as he disconnected the phone and wrapped the cord up. After he did that, he tucked it under his arm as he stood. "If you two will excuse me, I feel kind of drained, so I'm off to bed."

"Are you seriously taking the phone with you?" I asked him. I didn't like the fact that the only way we could communicate with the outside world was going to be locked up in the owner's room downstairs, not that there was anyone I needed, or even wanted, to call at the moment.

"Sorry, but I don't want any of them stirring up trouble while I'm resting," he told us.

"I get that," I said. "Will you at least *think* about going to see your daughter in the morning on that anniversary?"

Killian just shrugged, and then he followed us out of his office. He deadbolted the lock on the door, and I could see that it was pretty hefty. Nobody was going to be able to break in there without raising a ruckus, which I was sure had been his intent.

"Sleep well, old friend," Jake said as Killian headed for the downstairs door.

"If only I could," he said, and I saw him falter a bit before he caught himself.

As he vanished, I saw Jasper and Beatrice coming down the steps of the main stairway.

As she headed straight for his office door, I couldn't resist taking a shot at her. "Don't bother. He's not there."

"What do you mean, he's not there?" she asked me indignantly as she rattled the doorknob. I'd been right; it was firmly secured in place and barely moved under her onslaught.

"Gone, disappeared, left, vacated," I said with a smile that had no warmth to it at all. Her chilling words earlier were still on my mind, and I had no desire to even pretend to be cordial to her.

"I need to make a call," she insisted.

"Even if you could get inside, which you can't," Jake explained, "he took the only telephone with him to bed."

"We'll just see about that," Beatrice said as she started for the downstairs door.

"I wouldn't do that if I were you," Jake said coolly, the authority thick in his voice.

"Trust me when I tell you that what you would or would not do is no concern of mine," she snapped as she went to the door.

To the surprise of all of us, it was locked as well.

"This is ridiculous!" she snapped. "Come on, Jasper. We're leaving."

To my surprise, her brother didn't move. "No."

It was obvious that Beatrice wasn't used to hearing that word, and I had to fight the temptation to define it for her as well. "What do you mean, no?"

"I'm not driving down that mountain in the dark, and since you rode with me, you're stuck here until morning," he said.

"When did you suddenly grow a backbone?" she asked. "Give me the keys, then. I should have known you wouldn't be man enough to back me up."

"I'm not going to let you kill yourself, either," Jasper said. "Just take a second and breathe, Beatrice."

"Killing myself is exactly what I should do!" Beatrice looked at her brother as though she wanted to commit murder, not suicide, and if we hadn't been there as witnesses, she might have taken a stab at it, but after a moment she turned on all of us and trounced up the stairs, no doubt heading for her room to get her pout on.

"Sorry about my little sister," Jasper said. "She's a little high-strung."

Wow was that a massive understatement. "How do you manage?" I asked him gently.

"Oh, she's not *always* like this," he said. "I'd better go check on her, though. She's had a history of threatening to harm herself, and I don't want it to be because of me if she ever actually does it," Jasper added as he followed her.

I had a feeling that Beatrice would only threaten suicide if it would get her attention, but after she was gone, I began to wonder. "Jake, is there a chance she might actually be desperate enough to kill herself?"

"I don't think so," Jake said.

"But you don't know for sure," I replied.

"No, but if she's intent on it, there's nothing *we* can do to stop her," he answered.

It was kind of a cold response from him. "Are you okay?"

"I'm fine. I just don't have much patience for people who have everything, and it's still not enough. Leandra is fighting for her life with every ounce of her energy, and it cheapens her battle when people like Beatrice threaten to end it all just for the attention. I know that depression and despondence and desperation are all very real—trust me I've gone through them all—but what I can't abide by are people who *pretend* to be suicidal for the show of it."

I knew that he was talking about his own experiences after he lost his late wife and unborn daughter, and I understood why he felt the way he did. I'd lost a classmate, more than that, a friend, in high school to depression, and it had left an indelible mark on me. I'd tried to persuade her to get some help, but I hadn't tried as hard as I should have, and I would take that regret with me to my grave.

"What were all of those hysterics about?" Vera asked as she came down to join us in front of the fireplace.

"It sounded like a family thing to me," I said, not wanting to go into any details with her about our conversation with Killian's family. "Where's Abel?"

"How should I know? I'm not his keeper," she snapped.

"Sorry," I replied, though I really wasn't sorry at all. She'd gotten a little sympathy from me after the way Abel had threatened her, but she'd quickly used that up. Vera seemed like someone who might often inspire mayhem against herself.

"What are we supposed to do now? Is *he* holed up in there?" she asked as she pointed toward Killian's office.

"No, *he* went to bed," I said, using her same inflection.

Vera tried the door and was upset to find that it was locked. "I absolutely *hate* locked doors!" Were we really going to have to go through this yet again? "I have to get in there. I need to make a phone call."

"Sorry. It's going to have to wait until morning," I told her. "Killian took the phone with him to bed."

"It figures," she said with disgust. Outside, the wind began to howl and I could hear rain pelting against the glass at the balcony despite the overly generous overhang. "At least we still have power," she said.

A moment later we didn't though, as we were all plunged into darkness.

Chapter 8

"COME ON. SERIOUSLY?" Vera asked.

"At least we have the light from the fire," I told her. I wasn't in the mood to be completely plunged into darkness in a strange place where there was so much animosity in the air, either.

"I saw some candles earlier," Jake said as he made his way to the bench in front of the fireplace. Sure enough, under it were a dozen candles and holders for them as well.

"How did I miss these?" I asked him as he got out the tapers, and then retrieved a pack of matches as well.

"I wouldn't have seen them either if I hadn't had to bend over and tie my shoe earlier," he answered with a grin as he lit one and handed it to me. "I have a hunch this isn't the only stash. You heard Killian before. The power is an issue right now."

"Hey, I need one of those," Vera said impatiently.

Jake looked at me for a second before seating another candle and handing it to her. He was reaching for the matches when she said, "Give me the matches. I need a light."

"I'm working on it," Jake said, and I could swear he slowed down under her prodding. It was all I could do not to burst out laughing. When he finally managed to light a match, he 'accidently' dropped it on the floor, extinguishing it in the process. "Oops," he said.

"Give me those," she said as she tried to grab the box only to find that it was no longer within her reach. If she'd had any doubts earlier about Jake's reflexes, they were certainly gone now.

"I can do it. Just give me a second," Jake said. He lit another match and then made a show of lighting Vera's candle, but she still wasn't satisfied. She reached down and grabbed half the remaining candles and headed back for the stairs.

"Hold on. We might need those later," I told her.

"Tough. You should have been quicker," Vera crowed. "It's everyone for themselves."

Once she was gone, Jake said, "Good riddance."

"Even though she took half of our supply?" I asked, wondering about the petty ruthlessness of the woman.

"That's just half of what I pulled out." Jake grinned at me as he retrieved another full box of tapers. "We're all set."

"It shows you what kind of person she is, though, doesn't it?" I asked him.

"I believe we already knew that," Jake answered as he set up the rest of the candles and holders. "Shall we deliver these to the rest of the guests, since our host hasn't come back upstairs?"

"Beatrice already thinks I'm on the staff, so I'd hate to disappoint her," I answered.

Jake grabbed three holders with candles while I took ours, along with extra tapers as well. "Why don't you grab a few packs of matches, too?" he asked.

"You had more of those all along as well?" I asked. "Why did you make such a show of having to light Vera's candle for her and not giving her a pack of her own?"

"She had to pay a jerk tax for the way she was behaving, didn't she?" Jake asked me.

"I'm not upset with that idea, to be honest with you," I said approvingly, then we made our way upstairs and started knocking on doors.

"Beatrice, it's Jake and Suzanne," I said as I knocked on her door, at first gently and then with a bit more force.

There was no response.

"Could she be in there sulking?" I asked Jake.

"I wouldn't put it past her," he answered as another door close by opened. Jasper walked out into the hallway, and I saw that he was wearing silk pajamas and some kind of kimono. It didn't surprise me a bit that he also had on leather slippers, and I was honestly a little surprised he wasn't sporting a nightcap as well.

"What's going on here?" Jasper asked. Had we actually woken him? It was my bedtime as a donutmaker, but I didn't realize anyone else followed my crazy schedule.

"The power's out," I said, which was one of the more obvious statements I'd ever made in my life.

"I can see that," he answered, "but that still doesn't explain why you are trying to knock my sister's door down."

"She's going to need a candle if she's going to find her way around," I explained.

"If I know Beatrice, she's already taken enough sleeping pills to knock out a horse. You'd have better luck waking a stone than rousing her. Leave it with me. When she wakes up and sees that the power is out, she'll come find me first thing."

I wasn't so sure of that, but then again, I didn't care enough about it to argue the point with him. Jake lit a taper in its holder and handed it the man, along with two packs of matches and an extra setup for his sister. I gave him a few of the unlit candles as backups and tried not to smile as he fumbled with the bounty we'd just bestowed upon him.

"Be careful. We don't want to burn the place down, now do we?" I asked him.

"I'm *always* careful," Jasper said with a hint of scold in his tone.

Of that I had no doubt. "Anyway, we just thought you'd like to have some light in case you needed it."

"How long is the power going to be out?" he asked me as though it were my fault somehow.

If my hands had been empty, I would have been tempted to hold them up to my temples and pretend to concentrate. As it was, I had to fight every impulse I had to give him the smart-aleck answer his question deserved. "Who knows?"

He didn't seem all that pleased with my answer as he made his way back into his room. Jake wasn't going to let that stand, though.

He put his foot in the doorway so Jasper couldn't close it. "It's customary to say thank you when someone does you a favor."

Jasper looked as though he were about to snap back at Jake when he must have seen the expression on my husband's face. "Thank you," he said, barely able to get the words out.

Jake gave him a cold smile. "You are welcome," he said calmly as he withdrew his foot. It was clear it was all Jasper could do not to slam it in our faces, but prudence must have won out because at the last second, the velocity he'd put on it eased to a gentle push.

"That went well, didn't it?" I asked Jake with a smile. "You know, you'd probably have more luck teaching a horse to sing than getting that man to be polite."

"I know, but I owe it to the world to at least try," Jake said with the hint of a smile. "That covers Vera, Jasper, and Beatrice, so we only have one left up here."

"Abel," I agreed as we made our way down to his room.

Vera came to the door when we knocked, though. "What do you two want now?" she asked, clearly irritated by our very presence.

"I thought this was Abel's room," I asked as I tried to peek inside around her. "He's not in there too, is he?"

"Gross," she said. "Of course not. He didn't like this room and I didn't care, so we switched. It's all perfectly innocent." Vera glanced at our full arms. "So, you found more supplies. Good for you."

"We did," Jake said, still refusing to offer her any matches of her own. "Good night."

"Good night," she said with a frown as she slammed her door. At least she'd had the spirit to do it in our faces, unlike Jasper's tepid close.

"Who is slamming doors at this time of night?" Abel asked as he came out of his room, still fully dressed.

"The power's out, so we thought we'd bring everyone candles," I volunteered.

"That was nice of you," he said as he took a set from us. "I told Killian it was a fool's errand building up here in the middle of nowhere, but the man hasn't taken my advice for a very long time."

I didn't like him talking about our host, and my new friend, that way. "Was it about the time you lost faith in him and sold your part of the grocery chain to him at a loss?" I asked.

Abel was clearly about to say something less than cordial to me when he must have caught a glimpse of the expression on Jake's face and thought better of it. "There are two sides to every story, Ms. Hart. I'm sure Killian's version of what happened paints him in a rather better light than what really happened."

"So set us straight. What really *did* happen?" I asked him.

Abel started to tell me—I could see it in the way he braced himself—but then he clearly decided against it. "What does it matter anymore? It's water under the bridge at this point."

"And over the dam, too," I replied.

"What? What dam?" he asked, confused.

"The one right after the bridge," I explained patiently, as though he were unable to grasp the concept.

"Good night," Abel said, finally deciding that he was better off just dismissing us.

"Night," I said with a grin, and then turned to my husband. "It's true what they say, isn't it?"

"Some of it," Jake answered as we made our way back to the main level. "What are you talking about specifically?"

"No good deed goes unpunished," I answered. "Maybe we should have let them all just stumble around in the dark."

"Maybe we should have," Jake answered when I saw him stiffen up and shove the candles at me. The moment his hands were free I saw him reach for his handgun, so I looked in the direction he was staring.

We weren't alone anymore.

Someone was sitting in front of the fire with his back to us.

"It's just Hank," I told Jake softly the second I recognized the outline of the big man.

It was clear from his initial reaction that Jake was on edge, and as he put his weapon back in its holster, he said, "Better safe than sorry, you know?"

"I do," I said.

"What are you two whispering about in the dark back there?" Hank asked us with a smile as he turned around.

"The power outage," Jake said, covering for his earlier action of drawing on the handyman.

"It's a part of life on the mountain," Hank said with a sigh. "Hope you don't mind, but I got soaked out there trying to check things out, and there's no power in my apartment. I told Killian I wanted a wood stove with an oven, but it hasn't come in yet. As it is, I'm going to freeze to death down there."

"You could always sleep by the fireplace. That's what we're thinking about doing," I said, wondering if Jake and I should do that as well.

"No need for you to. It hasn't gotten cold up here, has it?" he asked with a grin.

I realized he was right. Though the temperatures were surely dropping outside, inside the structure was still quite warm. "What's that all about?"

"Killian put some kind of state-of-the-art geothermal something in. I don't understand how it works, but it's supposed to keep chugging along no matter what happens to the power. I'm not allowed to work on it, but I don't mind in this case."

"But it doesn't extend to your apartment?" Jake asked him. "How about downstairs?"

"The boss is safe and as snug as a bug in a rug, don't you worry about him," Hank said. "I'm guessing he doesn't even know the power's out. He's been sleeping a lot lately, and honestly, just between you and me and the walls, I'm worried about him."

The concern Hank had for his employer was obvious. "What exactly is going on with him, Hank?" Jake asked earnestly.

"I wouldn't have said anything, but I know what a high regard he has for you, sir," Hank said. "Leandra's not going to be able to hold on much longer, and when she goes, I'm afraid it's going to kill him. He told me one night last week when we were up here all alone that she's been the only thing keeping him going lately."

I felt my heart go out to our host again, and frowned when I thought about the lack of support he had around him. "I think you're the only one up here on his side," I told Hank as we took seats by the fire ourselves.

"Besides the two of you, you mean," Hank said. "You made his week cooking that meal with him. You know that don't you?"

"It was just dinner," I said, uncomfortable with the praise.

"It was a whole lot more than that, and you know it," Hank said. "I just wish I had better news for him when he wakes up in the morning."

"Is the power situation that bad?" Jake asked him.

"Not just the power, I'm afraid," Hank said with a frown.

"How much worse could it be?" I asked.

"The road down the mountain is completely gone."

Chapter 9

"IT'S GONE?" I ASKED loudly. "What do you mean, it's gone?"

"The last storm we got a few hours ago took care of what the weather's been trying to do for weeks," Hank explained. "The guy who cut in the new road cut some corners and decided not to put culverts in. Once the road started eroding, it was a losing battle. At the moment most of our road is lying at the bottom of the mountain, and there's no other way down."

I tried to take that in as Jake spoke. "So we're trapped here."

"There's no getting out in our vehicles for a while; that's for sure," he said.

"I'm surprised there isn't some other way down the mountain," Jake said.

"There is, if you don't mind hiking down a steep enough hill to kill you with one slip," he said.

"What about the phone line? Can we call someone for help?" I asked him.

"That line was in the same trench as the power was," Hank said as he shook his head. "Don't worry. We have staff coming in the morning, or at least that was the plan. When they see the road is out they'll get us help, so I wouldn't be surprised if they helicopter you all out of here by noon tomorrow."

"What about you?" I asked Hank.

"Oh, I'll stay here and keep working on the place. The truth of the matter is that I've got nowhere else to be," he said a bit too nonchalantly.

"I'm sorry," I said, letting the sympathy come through my voice.

"I appreciate that, but it's not necessary. I'm alone by my own stupidity, so it's nothing that I don't richly deserve." There was so much melancholy in his voice that I wanted to comfort him somehow, but

I honestly didn't know anything I could do. The moment passed, and Hank rubbed his hands together and tried his best to lighten his own mood. "I don't know about you two, but I could use a little toddy to take the chill off. Anyone care to join me?"

"What did you have in mind?" Jake asked him.

"Well, I haven't had a drink in seven years, eight months, and three days, but that doesn't mean I can't have a cup of hot chocolate to take the edge off."

"I'd be glad to make some, but how can I do it without power?" I asked him.

"The kitchen runs on propane," Hank said with a smile.

I'd seen some hot cocoa mix when I'd been in the kitchen working on dinner, so I stood and said, "I'll get started on it."

"I'll keep you company," Jake said as he joined me.

"Well, if you don't mind three being a crowd, all in all, I'd rather be in the kitchen with you folks than out here all by myself," Hank said. "This isn't a night to be alone with your thoughts, if you know what I mean."

Jake put a hand on the big man's shoulder. "I do."

Hank didn't pull away. "I could tell that about you. You've lost folks you care about too," he said. "Thanks."

"Let's go then, shall we?" I asked as cheerfully as I could manage amid the sadness.

"Lead the way, kind lady," Hank said.

I grabbed my candle, the other two did the same, and we made our way into the kitchen.

As I got started on warming the milk for the hot chocolate on the cooktop, Hank walked to the kitchen window. "There's a fog rolling in along with this rain. We're in for some rough weather before it gets any better," he said. "That might stop the helicopter from coming for us, but we've got plenty of food, we're warm, and we're dry, so there are a lot worse places we *could* be."

"I'd say that's looking on the bright side of things," I told him as I stirred the milk to keep from scalding it. While I did that, Jake got out three hefty mugs and some spoons.

"Where's the cocoa mix?" he asked me.

"Third cabinet, middle shelf, over there," I said as I pointed to the pantry.

"How did you happen to remember that?" Hank asked me with a curious look.

"Some people have photographic memories; I've got a foodographic one," I said with a smile.

"I'd say that all in all, that's a handier one to have," he answered as Jake followed my directions and retrieved the cocoa mix. "I've never heard of this brand," he said as he read the label out loud.

"It's French," I told him, having recognized it earlier. "I never thought I'd get a chance to taste it even when we went to Paris on our honeymoon."

"Nothing but the best for the boss," Hank said proudly.

"Has he always had such expensive tastes?" I asked.

Hank laughed. "When we first met, we shared a sandwich he'd packed himself for lunch. The man has had beer taste on a champagne budget for most of the time I've known him."

"So what changed?" I asked him as I poured the warmed milk into the mugs. The aroma of the chocolate was enough to make my mouth water before I even tasted a sip.

"Leandra got sick," he said plainly.

"I'm willing to bet that's what made him sell the company," I said.

"You got it in one. He decided life was too short, so he was going to make sure that his daughter was able to enjoy every last minute she's got," Hank answered soberly.

"Is it really that bad?" I asked him as I handed him his mug.

He took a sip and nodded. "That hits the spot," he said. "Yeah, I'm afraid she's not long in this world. The boss has her isolated from the outside world, terrified that she'll catch the sniffles from someone that pushes her over the edge. I doubt more than two people have seen her besides her doctors in the past three months."

"I'm kind of surprised he planned this outing then," I said as I took my first sip. It was amazing, as different layers of chocolate exploded on my tongue. I wasn't sure how much this stuff cost by the ounce, but whatever it was, it was worth it.

"I was too, to be honest with you, but it sounded like it was all Leandra's doing. She knew what kind of pressure everyone was putting on her dad, and she urged him to put an end to it once and for all so he could have some peace. The boss threw it together three days ago and insisted that everyone on his invitation list come, or else."

"So we weren't a last-minute addition?" Jake asked the handyman.

"I wish I could tell you that you were at the top of his list, but as a matter of fact you were the last ones he called. It kind of surprised me, to be honest with you. No offense."

"None taken," Jake said. "I wonder why it was so important that *we* come?"

"Maybe he wanted a few friendly faces around to take the sting out of his other guests," I said as I took another sip. I was going to have to slow down or I would need another cup soon, which wasn't the worst thing in the world.

"It wouldn't surprise me in the least, but I honestly couldn't say," Hank answered as he polished off his own mug. "That's a bit above my pay grade. The boss points me in the right direction and tells me what to do. Truth be told, I like it that way."

"You're extremely loyal to him, aren't you?" I asked Hank.

"I'd die for that man," he said, and then he smiled as he added, "Let's just hope it doesn't come to that." Hank put his mug in the sink and then thanked me. "That was amazing. Now, if you two don't mind, I'm going to go down to my place and change into some dry clothes."

"We don't mind at all," I said.

And that was when we heard a scream.

Chapter 10

"WHO WAS THAT?" I ASKED as we all rushed with our lit candles out of the kitchen and into the living room.

"It sounded like a man, so I'm guessing it was either Abel or Jasper," Jake said as he pulled out his handgun.

"Whoa there, partner. Is that really necessary?" Hank asked.

"I don't know yet. Let's go find out, shall we?" Jake asked as he rushed up the stairs.

It only took a second to realize where the scream had come from.

Beatrice's door was standing wide open.

Jake took the lead, though Hank and I were both close on his heels.

Jasper was standing at the window looking down. This side of the structure had an actual small balcony on every room, and the French doors had been thrown open.

"It's Beatrice!" he shouted as he pointed below us.

The fog was indeed rolling in, but I could still make out the figure on the rocks twenty feet below us.

It appeared that Beatrice had finally followed through on what I had assumed had just been an empty threat.

From the way she was laying there, there was no doubt in my mind that she had succeeded in the attempt to end her own life.

"We have to help her," Jasper whimpered as he stood there in the growing rain and expanding fog.

"There's nothing we can do for her," I said as I put a hand on his shoulder and started to pull him back inside.

He wasn't having it, though, and I was surprised by how strongly he was able to resist. "I'm going down there!"

Jasper started for the door when Jake and Hank both intervened.

"You're not going anywhere," Hank said.

"We can't just leave her down there," Jasper cried out.

Jake was about to say something when Hank spoke up. "He's right. From here we can't be sure that she's really dead. I'll go check on her."

"You can't do that," I told Hank. "It's too dangerous."

"I have a way down there that should be okay," he answered. "Jasper's right. We have to make sure she's not still alive."

"I'll go with you," Jake said.

Before I could protest, Hank replied, "As much as I appreciate the offer, I can't be worrying about you while I'm trying to climb down those rocks. I've got a rope I might need to pull her back up if she survived the fall, but I'm going to need you on the other end of it."

I knew that Jake didn't like to stand back while someone else did the dirty work, but what Hank suggested made sense. "Do it his way, honey."

Jake nodded. "You're the boss."

"Don't say that even as a joke. There's only one boss around here," Hank said. "Come on, let's go."

As we left the room together in a hurry, Vera came rushing out of her room, her candle sputtering so much that it almost went out. "What is all this nonsense about? I'm trying to sleep here!"

"We've got bigger problems than you getting your beauty rest," I snapped at her. "Beatrice has been hurt." I had a feeling that she'd been much more than injured in the fall, but I didn't want to get too graphic with Jasper right there beside me.

"What happened to her?" Vera asked, but I chose to ignore her. When she saw us rushing down the stairs, she said, "Suit yourselves. I'm going back to bed."

Nobody responded.

Once we were outside, it seemed as though the rain was picking up even more. "Is it really safe to go down there?" I asked as I looked down the twelve feet remaining where Beatrice lay.

"I'll be okay," Hank said. "While I'm climbing down, Jake, would you get the rope stashed away in the mudroom? It's under the bench marked *Outdoor Supplies*."

"I'm on it," Jake said as he vanished.

"I'm going with you," Jasper said, trying his best to act brave.

"If you do, then we're going to have more than one body to deal with tonight," Hank said shortly. "Stay here."

Jasper just whimpered.

"I'll make sure he doesn't try to follow you," I told Hank. "Be careful."

"You bet," he said as he started over the side of the cliff, choosing each foothold and handhold carefully.

He was almost to Beatrice when I saw the rock he was clinging to start to shift and break free from the cliffside.

"Hank!" I called out as he started to skid past the small outcropping where Beatrice lay.

He managed to grab the ledge as he slid past, and I didn't breathe again until he pulled himself up to lie beside her. "I'm okay!" he called up to us as Jake rejoined us, holding the rope.

"What happened?"

"The rock he was holding on to gave way, but he managed to save himself," I told him.

"How is she? Is she still breathing?" Jasper called out to Hank as he got to his hands and knees and leaned over the body.

After checking for a pulse for longer than I would have, Hank looked up at us and shook his head twice.

That's when Jasper fainted.

"Should we go ahead and haul her up?" Jake asked as he called down to Hank.

"I don't think we should risk it," Hank said, "but if you want to give it a shot, I'm game. The boss made me take a CPR class when he started building this place, so I know what to look for when I'm checking for a pulse. Still, I could be wrong."

"Let's try it," Jake said after a moment.

"You bet," Hank said as he tied the rope around Beatrice's shoulders and across her chest. "Wait till I get up there so I can help you."

"Should you use the rope to climb up first yourself?" I called down.

"No, it's liable to be more trouble than it's worth," he said. Hank made it back up the side of the cliff without incident, and then the three of us pulled Beatrice's body up. Jasper was no help at all, which I could forgive him for this time.

Once we got her body over the edge of the cliff, Jake knelt down to confirm Hank's diagnosis. "You were right. She's gone."

Jasper started weeping as he threw himself onto his sister's body. Evidently he'd come around while we'd been untying her. "Beatrice, why? Why would you do this?"

I started to pull him away, and then Jake helped me. "Let's get you inside and wrapped in a warm blanket," I told the mourning man. "There's nothing you can do for her now."

"We can't just leave her out here like this in the rain," Jasper said softly.

"We won't," I answered. "Hank and Jake will wrap her up in a blanket and bring her inside," I said, and then the two men did just that. We put Beatrice back in her room and closed the windows and door, which was the best we could do for her at that point.

"I can't believe Killian and Abel haven't come out to see what's been going on," I said.

"Killian wouldn't be able to hear a gunshot from down there in the basement," Hank said, "but Abel should have at least poked his head out like Vera did."

"Maybe someone should check on him," I said, a sense of dread creeping through me. Why *hadn't* he come out of his room?

"I'll go look in on him," Jake said.

"I'm coming with you," I said.

Hank replied, "You two go do that, and I'll go downstairs and get the boss. He'll know what to do."

"But he locked the door behind him," I told Hank.

"Maybe so, but I've got a key to every lock on this mountain. We'll be right back."

"See you in a few," Jake said as he turned to me. "Are you ready, Suzanne?"

"Let's go," I answered.

The door to Abel's room wasn't locked, which kind of surprised me. He seemed the type to wear a belt and suspenders, so why would he go to sleep without securing his door? Jake reached over to flip on the light, but of course, there wasn't any power. He shrugged as he looked at me, and then made his way over to the bed.

It had been slept in, but it was empty now.

"Where is he?" I asked. "Do you think he heard the commotion outside and came out to see what was going on?"

"If he did, we would have run into him," Jake answered as he made his way to the closed bathroom door. "Abel, are you in there? We're coming in."

There was no answer, so Jake pushed the door open with his free hand.

Abel was lying there, sprawled out on the floor with a pill bottle clutched in his hand. Pills were scattered everywhere, but it appeared that he'd been too late to take any of his heart medication to do any good.

Jake knelt down and checked for a pulse for the second time in ten minutes.

"Are you getting anything?" I asked.

"No. I'm sorry. He's dead too, Suzanne."

"What is this place, cursed or something?" I cried out. Finding one body was bad enough.

Finding two was infinitely worse.

"It's okay," Jake said as he put his candle down on the vanity and put his arms around me.

"In what universe is *any* of this okay?" I asked him, starting to cry without even realizing that I was doing it.

"It's not, but there's nothing we can do about either one of them at the moment," Jake answered calmly. "Nobody knew that Beatrice was actually going to follow through on her threat, and the fact that Abel had another heart attack was purely a coincidence."

"You know how I feel about coincidences," I told Jake as I pulled away.

He looked shocked by the suggestion. "Do you think there's a chance that these aren't what they seem to be?"

"I don't know," I said as I wiped the tears from my face. "There was bad blood everywhere we looked this evening, and now two people are dead. What do you think?"

"I don't like it either," Jake answered after giving it a few seconds' thought. "But that doesn't mean that coincidences can't happen. Why would someone kill Beatrice *and* Abel at the same time?"

"I'm not sure, but I think it would be a mistake to just assume that these deaths are unrelated," I told him. "What do you think?"

"I think maybe you've been investigating murders too long. It's gotten into your head," Jake answered.

"Then I'm probably just overreacting?" I asked him.

"Maybe, but it won't hurt to assume that you're right, and that someone's killing guests up here and trying to make them look like something else entirely."

Chapter 11

"I GOT THE BOSS," HANK said as he came upstairs.

"I just can't believe she actually did it after threatening to all for these years," Killian said. It was clear that his niece's death had rocked him on his heels. "Thank you for retrieving the body."

"It was the least we could do," Jake said. "I'm afraid we've got more bad news for you."

"I can't imagine things getting much worse than this," our host said.

"Abel is dead, too," Jake told him.

Killian and Hank both looked at him as though Jake had just told an extremely bad joke, but when they saw the expression on his face, it finally started to sink in.

"No. I don't believe it. Why would *Abel* kill himself?" Killian asked.

"He didn't. It looks as though he had another heart attack, but we'll have to leave that for the coroner to decide," Jake explained.

"I want to see the bodies," Killian said stoically.

"Boss, there's no reason to put yourself through that," Hank said with obvious care for his employer.

"I disagree," Killian answered. "Jake, I need to see them for this to be real."

"I get that," my husband said. "I don't see what it could hurt."

We went into Beatrice's room with our candles and Killian saw the body laid out in a blanket. "Why is she covered up? Did the fall...mar her face?" he asked us chokingly.

"No, we did it out of respect for her," I told him. "We can unwrap her if you need to see her."

"I'm sorry, but it's the only way it's going to be real to me," he replied.

I started to unwrap the part of the blanket over her face when Jake gently pushed me aside. "I'll do it, Suzanne."

I didn't want to argue the point, so I stepped aside. I knew that Jake had dealt with more dead bodies in his life than I ever could, and I wasn't all that upset about not having to touch another one. He took off the part that covered her face and then stepped aside.

Hank didn't even look at her, and I couldn't bring myself to do it, either.

After a few moments, Killian touched her cheek lightly and said softly, "I hope you find the peace you were looking for but never found here."

It was touching and filled with sadness at the same time.

He took another moment staring at her, and then he turned back to us. "Now we need to go see Abel," he said.

As Hank led the way out of the room, I watched as Jake delicately covered Beatrice's face again. As he did so, he frowned for a moment, and I had to wonder what thought had just crossed his mind. Was he mourning the loss of the beautiful woman, or was it something else? I couldn't very well ask him at the moment, but I'd have to do so later.

We joined the other two in Abel's room and found them in the bathroom beside the body. "Should we move him onto the bed, too?" Hank asked as he started to grab the dead body.

"No, we need to leave him right where he is for the coroner," Jake said.

"Do we honestly even *need* a coroner? It was clearly a heart attack. I guess he didn't make it to his heart medication fast enough," Killian said as he played his candle over the spilled meds all over the floor.

"Most likely, it was, but we still shouldn't touch anything," Jake told them.

"We moved Beatrice," Hank reminded him.

"We did, but when you went down there, we couldn't be sure that she wasn't still alive. Besides, if we'd left her on that outcropping, Jasper would have tried to retrieve her body himself, and then we'd have three bodies on our hands instead of two," Jake said. "If I'd had my druthers we wouldn't have moved her either, but circumstances didn't give us much choice. Besides, I was afraid that ledge might give way and we'd *never* recover the body. This isn't ideal, but it's the best we can do."

"Jake, you don't think there's anything suspicious about what happened tonight, do you?" Killian asked him. "I find that impossible to believe. Abel had a bad heart, and everyone knew it."

"Coincidences happen," Jake explained, "but it won't hurt to follow procedure until we can get the police up here."

"Good luck with that," Hank said.

"Why is that?" I asked him.

"The only way *anyone* is getting up here is by helicopter, and if that fog stays as thick as it is right now, nobody's coming up here for at least a few days," he explained.

"That's entirely unacceptable," Killian said. "There has to be some way for us to get off this mountain."

"I nearly fell when I climbed down to check on Beatrice," Hank explained. "The odds of making it down the mountain with at least one of us dying is pretty high, and *none* of us may make it. The best thing, really the only thing, we can do right now is sit tight and wait for someone to come get us."

"I don't like it, but I know you're right," Killian said. He then turned to Jake. "In the meantime, what do we do?"

"I already closed Beatrice's door. We should leave this room and lock them both behind us."

"If you think it's necessary," Killian said. "Do it, Hank."

As we started to leave, Killian looked toward his dead business partner and said something so low I couldn't hear him.

"What was that?" I asked him.

"I didn't realize that I'd said it out loud. I just told him goodbye," Killian explained. "We were partners for a great many years. It was a complicated relationship, especially after he sold out his share to me, but he was still my friend."

"I'm sorry for both of your losses," I told him as we all walked out of the room together.

We stepped out into the hallway and the handyman took out his master keys and locked both doors. "Now what?" Killian asked us.

"We need to wake up Vera," I said. "She needs to know about Abel." I thought about how he'd threatened her earlier and realized that she might even be a little relieved by the man's death. It sounded cold and cruel, but he *had* threatened her, and if Jake and I hadn't come along when we did, who knows what might have happened?

I knocked on the door to her room, and to my surprise, she opened it immediately. She hadn't even had to unlock it. "What is all of the commotion about it? I'm sorry the young woman killed herself, but there's nothing anything any of us can do about it until the police arrive. I assume you've already called them?" she asked when she saw that Killian was with us. "By the way, I resent you taking the telephone to bed with you. I demand that you let me make a call right now."

"You can try, but the phone line and the road down the mountain are both gone," Killian told her.

She clearly didn't believe him. "Stop trying to put me off with your lies, Killian. You know that's not true."

Hank shook his head as he said, "You're welcome to go look yourself, but I wouldn't do it if I were you. There's a landslide where our access road used to be, and if you're not careful, you'll go down the mountain with what's left of it."

That seemed to convince her. "I can't believe this. What does Abel think about the situation?"

Nobody said anything right away, so I spoke up. "I'm afraid Abel's dead, too," I told her.

"That's ridiculous. Abel would *never* kill himself. He valued his worth too much to ever do that, and everyone knows it."

"It appears that his heart gave out," Killian said.

Vera didn't look happy, but she didn't seem to be particularly upset by the news, either. "Well, we all knew that it was just a matter of time. I suppose the news of Beatrice's suicide was more than he could take."

"That's the thing, though," I said. "As far as we know, he didn't even know it had happened."

"So his heart just gave out like that out of the blue?" Vera asked. "I suppose it makes sense. He has been under a great deal of strain lately," she added as she glanced at Killian. "Who knew it would be more than he could take, though."

Killian didn't rise to the bait, which I thought was the perfect answer to her jibe. "Should we all go downstairs and sit by the fire?" I asked.

"That's the best idea I've heard all night," Hank said. "I can add a few more logs to it, since I doubt anyone's getting much more sleep tonight."

"That's what we'll all do, then," Killian said.

Vera balked at the suggestion, though. "I quit taking orders from you a long time ago, Killian. I'm going be in my room until the police make it up here. I don't trust any of you."

"Suit yourself," Killian said, turning his back on her. "Suzanne, why don't we whip some food up? I could use a bite to eat since we're up anyway."

"How can you eat after what's happened?" Vera asked him with an accusing tone in her voice.

"Starving myself isn't going to do either of them any good," he answered, "but if you want to fast for the next three days until we get help up here, be my guest."

As we walked down the stairs, I noticed that Vera ducked into her room long enough to grab a robe, and then she joined us. I was dreading telling Jasper about another death when we got to the fireplace, but that clearly wasn't going to be an issue, at least not right away.

He was nowhere to be seen.

Had we just lost another member of this cursed weekend in the mountains?

Chapter 12

"WHERE'S JASPER?" I cried out as everyone stared at me. "We left him right here."

"He was still sitting there when we came upstairs," Hank said, clearly looking confused about the situation.

"I tried to talk to him on our way up to you," Killian added, "but I could swear he was catatonic. Where could he be?"

I had a suspicion that I hoped wasn't true. "Could he have tried to get off the mountain despite what you told him about the road?" I asked Hank.

"If he did, then he's a bigger fool than I gave him credit for," Hank said as he raced out front with the rest of us close on his heels.

"His car's gone," Killian said as he peered out into the gloom. The light from our candles had a weird effect in the foggy night, making things look almost surreal.

"We have to find him," Jake said.

"Good luck with that," Hank said as he pointed in the direction of the road. "If he tried to drive down that landslide, they'll be digging his body out in the morning." He glanced Killian, who was looking at him oddly, and quickly added, "No offense intended, Boss."

"We need to go see," Jake interjected. "We have to at least be sure."

Vera shivered in the mist. "I'm not going out there in that mess. I'll be by the fire, where any sensible person would be on a night like tonight, if you need me."

"Fine. We'll see you later," I said as I started out into the parking lot.

"You don't have to come with us, Suzanne," Killian said.

"I know I don't have to. I need to."

He shrugged. "Then let's get going."

Hank led the way, Killian was beside him, and Jake and I took up the rear. It was tough seeing through the fog at times, and at others, it seemed as though it had parted just for our passing. The next moment though, it would be back in full force, and I wondered what chance Jasper would have driving in those conditions.

We found the car.

But it was empty.

Had Jasper gone as far as he could behind the wheel and then taken off on foot the rest of the way?

Or was he somewhere else on the mountain, lost in the fog and in danger of plunging off the side of the cliff with every step he took?

Chapter 13

"JASPER! JASPER!" I called out.

"What are you doing, Suzanne?" Killian asked me.

"If he's lost somewhere, he may be able to follow my voice," I explained before calling out to him again.

"I don't blame you for trying, but the odds are one in a thousand he's still alive," Hank told me. "I'm sorry, but I think you're wasting your breath."

"Maybe so," I said, and then I called out again, "Jasper!"

Jake joined in, and Killian did, too. Hank shrugged and started calling out for the man himself. I thought I heard something, but with everyone yelling it was hard to tell. "Everyone shut up for a second!" I ordered.

They all did as I'd ordered, and then, in the eerie silence of the night, I heard a voice call out. "I'm down here."

The good news was that Jasper was still alive.

The bad news was that he was pretty far below us, down the mountainside and deep into the belly of the mist.

"Jasper, keep talking so we can find you," Hank said, getting into the spirit of the thing. "We're coming to get you."

"You didn't tell me how bad the road really was," Jasper accused Hank. "I nearly died."

"I told everybody that the road was gone!" Hank said, clearly exasperated about being blamed for Jasper's current predicament. "I did everything but take your car keys from you and throw them over the side of the cliff!"

Killian put a hand on Hank's arm. "Don't take it personally. It's just the way Jasper is. Nobody blames you for this."

"I don't see how they could," Hank said, clearly bewildered by his boss even saying something like that. "I didn't put that road in without a culvert, and I sure didn't make it rain hard enough to wash the side of the mountain away."

"Nobody said that you did," I told Hank, trying to settle him down. It was clear that the handyman was on the edge of losing it himself, and we didn't need any more breakdowns tonight. "Let's just concentrate on getting Jasper back."

Hank nodded, and I could see that my attempt had helped him get control of himself again.

"Can you at least walk?" Jake asked Jasper as we all started toward the sound of his voice.

"Yes, but I'm afraid I'm in a bit of a jam," Jasper said.

"Describe it to us," Killian ordered.

"I was going for help," Jasper whined. "Beatrice needs to get off this mountain."

I wasn't sure what I expected from Killian, but he was fairly calm as he said, "That's what we're going to try to do as soon as we can, but for now we need to get you back up here with us where it's safe. Keep talking."

"I slid down a ways," Jasper explained. "I tried to climb back up, but I wasn't strong enough."

That didn't surprise me, since I'd noticed from the first moment I'd met him that Jasper wasn't all that fit.

"Don't worry. We'll be there soon," Killian said, comforting him as best as he could, and then he turned to Hank and asked softly, "Is there any chance we can get to him where he is?"

"I wish I'd brought that rope with me," Hank conceded.

"I can go back and get it," I volunteered as I started back into the fog.

"You don't need to be going anywhere," Jake said as he reached out for my arm. "We can figure something out, but what I can't afford is you wandering off into this fog and falling yourself."

"I can find the house. I think," I said as I glanced back in the direction I believed we'd just come.

But I couldn't be sure. The fog just might end up killing us all before the night was over.

Everyone but Vera, whose decision to stay behind was beginning to seem like the smartest thing any of us could have done.

"Let's all hold hands," I said. "That way, if one of us stumbles, the others can keep them from falling."

"I don't think we need to do that," Hank said, clearly uncomfortable about the idea. "Besides, what would we do about our candles?"

"The fog above is starting to break up a little, and we're in luck," I said. "There's a full moon tonight. We'll have enough light to see by. Besides, there's too much of a chance we'll all end up like Jasper if we don't." When he still hesitated, I put my candle out and stuffed it into my back pocket. The holder wouldn't fit in, but at least enough of it would go in to keep it from falling out of my pocket. "You can hold on to yours if you want, and Killian can keep his, too. That should be enough to see by. Come on. I'll take your hand, you big sissy," I told him as Jake grabbed hold of my other one.

Killian had no problem taking Jake's hand, and we walked side by side forming a human chain, with one light in front and one in the rear.

"Keep talking," I called out to Jasper.

"I'm getting hoarse," he said, whimpering a bit. "I'm freezing, too."

"You'll be wrapped up in a blanket sitting by the fire soon enough," Killian told him. "Tell us about your rock collection." He then added softly to us, "It's the only thing I've ever seen him passionate about. In fact, I've never been able to get him to shut up about it."

"They're called geodes," Jasper said in a condescending manner.

"My mistake," Killian said, and I could see his grin in the moonlight. "What exactly is a geode again? I forget."

"Seriously? I've shown you my collection a dozen times. Weren't you paying attention?"

"Humor me," Killian said as we got closer and closer to the voice lost in limbo.

"In layman's terms, it's a cavity in a rock, usually quartz, that's filled with crystals or minerals," he explained. "But that does nothing to explain their brilliance, variety, and beauty."

"Tell us more," I said.

And then the earth fell out from under my feet.

Chapter 14

"HANG ON, SUZANNE. I've got you," Jake said as my feet were suddenly dangling out over space. "Hank, do you have that side?"

"Yep, but I'm starting to slip myself," he said. "Help me get her back up here with us."

I tried to help them, but there was nothing under me to allow me to fight the pull of gravity down into the fog.

Suddenly I felt myself being pulled upward, and a moment later I was on solid ground again. It was all I could do not to collapse in a heap, and if it hadn't been for Hank and Jake still holding on to me, I might have done just that.

Once we were ten steps away from the edge of the precipice, I let go of Hank's hand and threw myself into Jake's arms. He stroked my back as I clung to him for dear life, not afraid of falling, but afraid of what might have happened if we all hadn't been holding hands.

"It's okay," Jake said softly in my ear. "You're okay now, Suzanne."

"I know. I thought I was lost for a second there, though."

"I would *never* let that happen," Jake said, and I believed him.

"What do we do now?" Killian asked. "I'm not sure it's safe for us to climb down there together and get him."

"There's only one thing we *can* do," Hank said. "If we go back for that rope, we may never find him again, or be too late to help him. He's going to have to climb up himself."

"I can't see that happening," Killian said. "He's not strong enough."

"He might just surprise you," I said. "Besides, what choice do we have?"

Killian nodded, and after looking at the others, I realized it was going to be my job to coax him up the hillside.

"Jasper, it's too dangerous for us to climb down to where you are," I told him, fighting to keep my voice calm.

"You're going to just leave me here to die?" he asked, the panic thick in his voice.

Killian started to reply when I shook my head. The two men had a combative relationship, and what we needed now was cooperation. "We're not leaving you," I told him soothingly. "You have to come to us, though."

"I can't," he said, whimpering a bit as he spoke.

"You can. You have to do this, for Beatrice," I said.

It was probably a low blow using the man's dead sister as motivation, but honestly, what else did I have in my arsenal? He wouldn't do it for Killian, for himself, or even his precious geodes, but I had a feeling he would try to move mountains for his sister. After all, hadn't that been what had gotten him into this mess in the first place? "Come on. Follow my voice," I said.

"Why are you the only one talking to me? Did the others abandon me?" he asked.

"We're still here," Jake said.

"Nobody's going anywhere," Hank added.

"I'm here, too," Killian said.

That seemed to buoy his spirits. "Do you really think I can do this, Uncle K?"

He looked at me and shrugged. "The truth is, I don't," Killian said softly.

"Then lie to him and tell him what he wants to hear," I said fiercely.

"You bet," Killian answered loudly with more enthusiasm that I thought he had in him. "You can do it!"

That seemed to be the last nudge Jasper needed. "Okay. I'm going to try." After a few seconds he said, "Keep talking, Suzanne. It's helping."

"I had some geodes when I was a kid," I said. "They're really cool, aren't they?"

"Are you telling me the truth, or are you just trying to make me feel better?" he asked me from below us. I heard some scraping noises coming from him too, so I knew that he was doing his best to join us.

"I'm sure they weren't as cool as your collection, but I went on a field trip to a gem and mineral show in school, and I bought a bag of geodes that hadn't been broken up yet. It was so cool using a hammer to crack them open. The ugliest rocks I'd ever seen suddenly transformed into ones with really cool crystals on the inside. They looked like miniature caves."

"You should see mine," Jasper said with pride as he continued to make his way up. "I've got one that's as big as a chair..."

His words were cut off as we heard him slide downward, and I wondered if that was the end of Jasper.

The main noises stopped, though I heard trickling sounds of dirtclods and rocks continue to fall even after he'd stopped himself. "Are you okay, Jasper?"

"I slipped a little," he admitted.

We'd gathered that much, but I couldn't afford to be sarcastic while a man's life might be hanging in the balance. "But you're not hurt."

"I'm pretty muddy, but other than that, I'm fine," he said, and to my amazement, I heard him begin his climb again. I thought for sure that the setback would rob him of his last bit of strength, but to my surprise, he somehow managed to keep climbing.

"Then just think about how great a shower is going to feel in a few minutes," I told him, doing my best to keep him climbing, no matter what.

"Yeah. I've forgotten what it's like to be warm and dry," he said.

Was he actually getting closer? I could hear his voice much more distinctly now. "You're doing it, Jasper. You don't have far to go now."

I wasn't positive that it was true, but I hoped it was.

Hank reached for my hand. "Come on. Let's see if we can pull him up the last few feet."

He started forward, but Killian balked. "He's my nephew. I'll do it."

"No offense, Boss, but I'm a bit stronger than you are," Hank said.

"I'm well aware of that fact, but he's nearly all that I've got left of family, and I'm not going to let anyone else down."

"There was nothing you could do about Beatrice," I told him, my heart breaking yet again for the man.

"I'm not sure that's true, but thanks for saying it," Killian said as he took over the lead despite Hank's earlier protests.

I looked at Jake, who just shrugged and went along with his friend. It wasn't the best way to save Jasper, but I could see it was the only thing Killian would allow.

"Feel for the edge of the cliff with your foot," Hank told his boss as Killian started off into the heavy fog. It was picking up again, and I had to wonder if our mission wasn't doomed to fail. "Be careful, okay?"

"I will be," Killian said softly. "Jasper, you're close. We're going to reach a hand out to help you, so when you see it, grab ahold of it."

"Is Hank strong enough to pull me up?" he asked.

"It's not going to be Hank, it's going to be me. *I'm* going do it," Killian said. "Come on up, boy."

That seemed to be all that Jasper needed to finish his ascent. Suddenly, I heard Killian cry out, "Take my hand in yours. I've got you!"

"I'm slipping!" Jasper shouted a second later, and it was clear to me that Killian was going to lose his grip.

Jake's hand let go of mine.

He quickly reached down to grab Jasper by his shirt collar and single-handedly pulled him up.

"I'm sorry. I thought I had you," Killian said. "I just lost my grip all of a sudden."

"No worries, Killian. We got him. That's all that counts," Jake said as he patted his friend on the back.

I saw the man my husband had just saved get on his hands and knees and pant heavily, broken from exhaustion and grief. It really had been that close, but Jasper was finally safe again.

As safe as any of us were at the moment, at any rate.

"It's getting c-c-c-colder," Jasper said as he shivered on our way back to the house.

It felt the same amount of chilly to me as it had before, but then again, I hadn't been out in the cold air and the rain like he had, either.

"Just remember what I said before and keep thinking about how good that shower is going to feel," I told him as we came into the parking lot and walked up the stairs.

"That's the *only* thing I'm trying to think about right now," Jasper said. "I still can't believe that Beatrice is gone."

"It's got to be tough, losing her like that," I told him.

"It is," he nodded as he looked at me. "Thanks for talking me up that hillside. I wouldn't have made it otherwise."

"You're most welcome," I said. "After you finish with your shower, come back downstairs and I'll make you some fresh coffee."

"That would be perfect," he answered as we all walked inside.

"What were you thinking, going out wandering around in the fog in the middle of the night? What kind of idiot does that?" Vera asked him as he walked past her.

If he heard her, he didn't choose to respond, which was probably just as well.

Once Jasper was upstairs, I said, "You could be a little nicer to him, you know? After all, he just lost his sister."

"So? I lost a friend and a business partner, but you don't see *me* going off the deep end," she snapped. "Why aren't you more torn up about Abel than you are, or your niece either, for that matter?" she asked Killian.

"The truth is that I've had so much death in my life that it doesn't seem to matter all that much to me anymore," he said sadly. "We're all going to die, and for most of us, it's going to be sooner than later."

"Wow, that's a cheerful thought," she said sarcastically.

"Take it easy, lady. He's had a tough time of it," Hank said as he started to walk toward Vera. He could be a large and menacing presence, and I could see Vera shrink back a little.

"I didn't mean anything by it," she said defensively. "This situation is a mess. At least we all should be able to agree on that."

"Nobody's arguing the point," Jake said. "Suzanne, is there any of that hot cocoa left?"

"No, but I promised Jasper coffee, so I can make some of each," I said.

"I'll join you," Jake answered.

"If it's all the same to you, I'll stay out here by the fire and warm up a little bit," Killian said.

"That sounds good to me, too," Hank added, looking at his employer worriedly.

"Well *I'm* not going anywhere, either," Vera said. "I didn't go out to find Jasper, and I'm not moving now. I just got comfortable."

"Fine. We shouldn't be long," I told them.

Jake and I disappeared into the kitchen, and as I started working on getting fresh beverages for everyone, I asked my husband, "Is Killian all right? He sounds like he's one good nudge away from following Beatrice over the rail."

"You know, I've been thinking about that," Jake said, "but I wanted to wait to talk to you until we were alone."

"Leandra's declining health has really gotten to him, hasn't it?" I asked. "He sounded really despondent in there just now."

"He did, but that wasn't what I was talking about," Jake said. "Did you get a good look at Beatrice's face when I uncovered it?"

"I just glanced at her, but she looked so peaceful it was almost as if she was sleeping, wasn't it?" Before Jake could reply, something suddenly occurred to me. "It shouldn't have looked that way though, should it? If she jumped, she would have hit face-first when she landed, but there wasn't a mark on her that I could see."

"The back of her head had a nasty dent in it, though," Jake said.

"But there wasn't enough room for her tumble and fall like that, was there?"

"No, I don't think so," Jake said firmly.

"Then that means that she didn't jump, or was even pushed," I said, putting it all together. "Someone must have clobbered her in her room and then chucked her over the side of the balcony. Throwing her out would have probably made her flip once on her way down, making her land the way she did. Jake, Beatrice didn't commit suicide, did she?"

"I think there's a good chance that she didn't," he said resolutely.

"Who would want to kill her, though? I know that she was annoying, but come on, murder?"

"The only suspect I can think of is Jasper," Jake said. "You heard how hard she went after him on the deck. Maybe he finally had all that he could take and pushed her back, literally."

"If that's true, then why did he try to go get help?" I asked, and then suddenly I knew the answer. "He wasn't going for reinforcements. He was trying to escape."

"I think it's a real possibility," Jake said. "We can't let that happen."

"Well, he's not going anywhere right now," I answered, feeling a twinge about being so nice to someone who might be a killer.

"No, but we can't let on that we suspect anything in the meantime," Jake said. "Can you do that, Suzanne?"

"No problem," I said.

He didn't accept that answer easily. "Really?"

"Okay, maybe a little problem, but I can do it. You can trust me, Jake."

"I know that. I do, with my life," he answered as he patted my shoulder.

The coffee and cocoa were soon ready, so I grabbed a tray and put the carafes on them, along with cups, spoons, some cream, and some sugar as well.

I didn't leave the kitchen, though.

"I just had a thought," I told Jake.

"It was bound to happen sooner or later," he answered with a slight grin. "Sorry, that was entirely inappropriate."

"Sure, but it was funny too, so I'll let it slide," I said. "Are we one hundred percent sure that Abel died of natural causes?"

"Why would Jasper kill a man he hardly knew?" Jake asked.

"He could have seen or heard something that implicated Jasper in his sister's death," I said, "or someone else might have done something to him. Do you remember how Abel nearly shoved Vera off the balcony before you could stop him? What if she decided to take matters into her own hands before he could make good his threat?"

"How would she do that?" Jake asked. "It seems as though Abel had a heart attack, at least based on the way we found him."

"But Beatrice seemed like a legitimate suicide at first too, didn't she?" I asked.

"We've got to get Hank's keys and check out Abel's room," Jake said.

"I agree, but how are we going to do that?"

"I'm not sure, but I won't be able to rest tonight until I know one way or the other," my husband answered.

"Either way, I'm sleeping with one eye open. I'd hate for Jasper to consider one of us a threat to his freedom," I said.

"Don't worry. I've got your back."

"And I've got yours," I replied.

Chapter 15

JASPER WAS ALREADY back downstairs when we came out of the kitchen, and it was all I could do not to stare at him as a potential killer, of his very own sister no less. Remembering my promise to Jake, I did my best to smile at him as I offered him the tray. "Did you have a good shower?"

"I'm still kind of numb from the cold, but it was nice to get clean and put on fresh clothes," he said as he took a mug and filled it with black coffee. I would have taken him for a cream-and-sugar kind of guy, but with the night he was having, maybe black coffee was the way for him to go after all.

"Ooh, cocoa," Vera said. "Bring me some of that."

I put the tray on the appropriately named coffee table. "Help yourself." I wasn't about to wait on her.

"Fine," she said, clearly a little disgruntled by my refusal to serve her. "I'll get it."

"That sounds good to me," I said, giving her my best fake smile that I reserved for only my worst customers at the donut shop.

"Where's Abel?" Jasper asked as he looked around the room. "Surely he couldn't be sleeping through everything that's happened tonight."

"That's right, you don't know, do you?" I asked, watching his face for some kind of sign that he indeed knew exactly what had happened to the older man. "Apparently, Abel had a heart attack around the time that your sister died."

"He's gone, too?" Jasper asked numbly. "You're kidding me."

"That's not something we'd joke about," Killian said.

"This place is cursed, Uncle K," Jasper said glumly, almost as though the last bit of fight had gone out of him. "Why did you ever build it in the first place?"

"I thought it would please Leandra," Killian said chokingly.

"And she's never even been up here to see it, has she?" Jasper asked harshly.

"Shut your yap," Hank said as he loomed over Jasper in a threatening manner. "Killian has enough on his mind without dealing with guff from you."

"It's okay, Hank," Killian answered. "He's right. I thought this would somehow make everything okay, but all it's done is to bring more grief into my life."

"Don't beat yourself up about it, Boss," Hank said as he laid a meaty paw on Killian's shoulder. It amazed me how gentle the big man's touch could be.

"I can't seem to help myself," Killian answered as he put a hand on his employee's hand. "Thanks for trying, though."

After a moment, Jasper said softly, "I'm sorry, Uncle K. I didn't mean anything by it."

"Don't worry about it," Killian said. He looked around at all of us for a moment, and then he stared at me for a second. "Suzanne, I know it's late, but I've got a hunch that none of us are going to be getting any sleep tonight. Is there any chance you could whip up that batch of donuts I've heard so much about from Jake that you promised us in the morning?" He had an imploring expression on his face, and I couldn't bring myself to say no, even though I was dog tired from everything that had happened, and it was so far past my bedtime it was time for me to get up again if I were back home running Donut Hearts, something that I wished I was doing with all of my heart and soul.

"I'd be happy to," I said as I stood. "They won't be yeast donuts, but how does a batch of cake donuts sound to everyone?"

There were some nods and a few agreements, but nobody seemed all that enthusiastic about the prospect.

Given the circumstances, I could hardly blame anyone for not being more excited about the idea.

"I'll have them done in no time at all," I said.

"Should I help you?" Killian offered.

"You can if you want to, but I've got this recipe down cold. I run the donut shop by myself alone one day a week, so this will be old hat for me."

"Then maybe I'll stay out here by the fire if it's all the same to you," Killian said. "I could use a rest."

"By all means then, take it," I said. I glanced at Jake but didn't say anything, wondering if he'd volunteer to help so that we could brainstorm a little more while I fried donuts.

He got the message, even though he didn't accept my offer. "I think I'll hang out here too if you don't mind." It was clear that he didn't want to leave this gang unsupervised, and I couldn't really blame him, especially if there was one, or maybe even two, murderers on the loose. Staying together tonight might be the safest way we'd all get through it. It would mean that Jake and I couldn't go off on our own and investigate, but it also meant that the killer, or killers, would have a harder time striking if we were all together.

"Sounds good to me," I said as I made my way into the kitchen, alone.

I could light enough candles to give me plenty of illumination in the kitchen, and before long I had a basic cake donut recipe ready to fry. The only large pots they had were all La Cruesset, a brand of French cookware I'd never be able to afford if I lived to be a hundred. This cast-iron pot looked to be around six quarts, and it was coated in an orange and red enamel that was amazing. I started frying donuts and fishing them out, placing them on draining racks as I made them. It was a small batch, at least for me, so I only made four dozen, which should be plenty enough to satisfy this group. I sprinkled two dozen with powdered sugar, a dozen were glazed with a quick vanilla icing I made up, and I left the last dozen plain. Everybody should be able to find something they liked that way. I found a fancy serving platter and placed the donuts on them as best I could and then carried them out to where everyone was still gathered at the fireplace.

"Come and get them while they're hot," I said as I put the platter down.

"Are there any blueberry?" Vera asked as she studied my offerings critically.

"Nope, they're all just my basic recipe," I said, trying my best not to pick up a freshly powdered donut and hurl it at her.

"They smell amazing," Hank said. He grabbed a plate someone had put out and plopped three donuts, one of each kind, on it.

"Hey, save some for the rest of us," Vera complained.

"I didn't take a single blueberry donut, because there aren't any," Hank said as he laughed at her.

"There's plenty for everyone," I jumped in. "I made four dozen."

"That should cover me, but what about the rest of these guys? What are they going to eat?" Hank asked cheerfully.

"If you can eat all of those donuts by yourself, I'd be happy to make more," I told him with a grin.

"You just called my bluff, didn't you? Still, I'll try to do proud by you," Hank answered as he took a hefty bite of one of the powdered donuts. "I know you're married to that man over there, but is it a *happy* marriage? I might be able to sweeten the deal a little after tasting these."

"Sorry, but I'm *extremely* happy," I said as I smiled at Jake.

My husband shook his head in amazement. "I've never seen a man have the nerve to make such a blatant pass at another man's wife right under his nose in my entire life."

"Aw, I was just pulling your leg," Hank said sheepishly.

"Make sure that's all that you're pulling, and that it's *my* leg and not *hers*, and we'll be fine," Jake said with merely the hint of a smile.

Hank obviously read the meaning behind the message. "I read you, loud and clear."

"Good," Jake answered, and the tension, at least over that exchange, dissipated.

In the meantime, Killian took a bite of a plain donut himself, though it was a much more restrained one than his handyman had taken. "Simply amazing, Suzanne. This is even better than dinner was, if that's possible."

"Well, in my defense, I've had a lot more practice making these," I answered, giving him a gentle smile. I was happy that I had managed to take Killian's mind off his troubles, even if it was only for a minute. That was what my donuts were for, at least as far as I was concerned, making the world a little brighter for a brief moment. What more noble a calling was there than that?

We did a good job making a dent into the donut supply, and even Jasper and Vera ended up polishing off two apiece. I had to sample each one as my professional duty, or at least that's the lie I told myself as I wiped the powdered sugar off an index finger and a thumb.

Once we'd all had our share, we seemed to sink back into our seats and stare into the fire, lost in our own thoughts.

Maybe it wouldn't be so bad after all.

I felt that way, at any rate, until Jasper stood and said, "I need to see Beatrice."

"I'm sorry, but we've locked both rooms," Killian said.

"Why? What could it possibly matter at this point?" Jasper asked him.

"It was my idea," Jake volunteered. "I didn't want anyone disturbing anything until the local police get here to investigate."

Jasper looked shocked by the suggestion, but I had to wonder if his reaction was real or if had been staged for our benefit. "Why on earth would they need to do that? A despondent young woman killed herself and an old man with a history of heart problems had another episode. It's as plain and straightforward as that."

"Maybe yes, maybe no, but that's not our call to make," Jake said.

That got Killian's attention. "What are you implying, Jake?"

"I'm not implying anything," he told his friend carefully. "I'm just saying that as a former state police investigator, I would want the scenes left as untouched as possible so I could get a look at them myself."

"But you're not an investigator anymore, so what you think doesn't really matter," Vera snapped. "Jasper's right. Let him see his sister if he wants to. There's no reason to be so barbaric about it, or melodramatic. I hate locked doors! There's no need to go to such extremes."

Jake held his cool, which I knew that he was good at. I noticed that there were still a few powdered donuts left, so maybe I'd be flinging them in Vera's direction after all if she didn't do something about the tone she was using with my husband.

"I'm not being melodramatic," Jake said patiently. "It doesn't matter at this point what we believe. We just need to preserve both scenes as best we can and let the authorities handle it."

"Even though we moved Beatrice's body," Hank reminded him.

"Like I said before, I was afraid that outcropping might give way," Jake said. "I made a judgment call that I'm going to have to explain when law enforcement arrives, but I can live with that."

"I didn't mean anything by it," Hank said. "Do you really think there's been some monkey business on the mountain?"

"It's considerably more than monkey business if two people were murdered up here," I said, forgetting that I was supposed to be a calming influence, too.

"You know what I meant," Hank said apologetically.

"No one killed Beatrice," Jasper said. "Now, if someone doesn't let me into her room, I will break that door down myself."

The man ordinarily couldn't punch his way out of a wet cardboard box, but I wasn't entirely sure he couldn't do just what he'd threatened to, given the circumstances.

"What do you think, Jake?" Killian asked my husband. "Could it really hurt anything if he doesn't touch anything?"

"Maybe not," Jake answered, which kind of surprised me. Was he using Jasper's insistence as a way to get another look at that body himself? "Who else wants to come with us?"

"Why are you coming?" Jasper snapped out at him.

"It's the only way I'm letting you in to see her. You'll be supervised by me the entire time that you're up there," Jake said. "That point is not negotiable. Go or don't go, it's up to you."

Jasper turned to his uncle. "Tell him I don't need to be watched, Uncle K."

Killian seemed to think about it for a few moments before he shook his head. "Sorry, but I can't do that. Jake is right. I can't stand the thought of seeing Beatrice again, so if Jake can do it, it's more than I can ask of him. How about the rest of you?"

"I'm sticking with you, Boss," Hank said, surprising no one.

"I'm certainly not going to go look to satisfy some kind of morbid curiosity," Vera said as she looked with disdain at Jasper.

"Suzanne?" Jake asked me.

I couldn't read his signals on whether he wanted me to come with him or stay with the group, so I made a judgment call. "Why not? I'll keep you company," I said. I figured if the other three of our remaining members of our party stayed together, no one else would die.

At least that was my hope.

Jake didn't object to my plan, so that was something, but he did turn to the others. "I want the three of you to promise me that you'll stay right here until we get back."

"Is that strictly necessary?" Killian asked.

"If I have to stay down here to make sure that it happens, you need to realize that you'll be sending Suzanne up there with Jasper alone," Jake said levelly. "Is that really what you want?"

Killian got the message. "Of course not. We'll behave ourselves, right?"

Hank nodded, but Vera didn't say a word. Killian repeated loudly, this time staring straight at her, "Right?"

"Right," Vera said, clearly not willing to cross her old boss again.

"Go, but don't stay long," Killian said.

"We won't," Jake replied, and then he turned to Hank. "I'll need those keys, please."

"Right. I almost forgot I had them," Hank said as he fished two keys off his massive ring. "I'll be needing those back later."

"When we're finished with them," Jake answered.

As we climbed the stairs, Jasper asked Jake, "Why wouldn't you send your wife upstairs with me by herself?"

"The truth is that I don't like her going *anywhere* without me," Jake answered. "Viewing a dead body is especially something I don't approve of her doing solo."

Jasper seemed to accept that.

Once we were at Beatrice's door, Jake took one of the keys and opened the door, handing me his candle as he did so.

When he retrieved it, he slipped another key into my hand. "Check out Abel's room," he whispered. "Be quick about it. I don't want anyone to know what you're up to."

"What exactly am I looking for?" I asked him as I took it.

"I'm not really sure. Anything that could tell us what really happened to the man, I suppose," Jake said softly. "Good luck."

"You, too," I said. "Thanks for believing in me."

"Every day, in every way," he answered as he gave me a quick peck on the cheek.

"You'd better get in there," I said as I pointed to Beatrice's room. "I'll see you soon."

"I'm counting on it," he answered as he stepped inside.

That left me maybe three or four minutes to see if I could tell if Abel had really died from natural causes, or if someone had helped him on his way.

Chapter 16

IT WAS KIND OF EERIE being in a dead man's room, especially with him still occupying it, in the middle of the night with only a candle for illumination. Not that bright overhead lights would have helped anything, but still, the candlelight threw off some really creepy shadows, something I didn't need on a mission that was already spooky enough.

The last thing I wanted to check out was the body, so I decided to ease myself into it by looking at every other thing in the room possible first.

Abel's clothes had been neatly put away in the drawers, and nothing appeared to have been disturbed. He had an old-fashioned appointment book, one that had real pages and everything, instead of one that worked electronically. It didn't surprise me one bit that the man had been old-school.

I flipped through the book and found a series of appointments, all business, that included Vera at times, alone, and Killian alone as well. The last appointments listed were Vera at her place, Killian at his full-time home, and to my surprise, here on the mountain a few days before the rest of us arrived on the scene. It was only blocked in for an hour, and Abel had made some notes on the meeting, as was his custom after every appointment.

"Killian is being stubborn to the nth degree. Things got heated, and his handyman stepped in at one point. I had to at least try, didn't I? What is Killian doing out here in the middle of nowhere, anyway? He's not going to change his mind about buying the chain back, I know that now. Vera is wrong. I don't know how I'm going to convince her of that, though. What a mess. Maybe we can change his mind next week when we come back here with his worthless niece and nephew. If not, I'm going to have to deal with Vera myself."

So, pushing Killian was more Vera's idea than it had been Abel's. That last bit had sounded like an overt threat, and if Vera had been the one who'd died on the mountain, I would have made Abel my prime suspect. The reversed situation didn't make much sense, though.

Then I checked the notes for has last meeting with Vera.

"Vera isn't going to give up. I told her that I was out, but she won't let me walk away from it. I don't know how she uncovered what I did, but it's coming back to haunt me yet again. Maybe Killian will get rid of her for me so I won't have to worry about her anymore."

What did that mean? Had Vera been blackmailing Abel to get him to cooperate with her? It was looking more and more as though she was the mastermind in trying to get Killian to go back to work.

I realized that I was running out of time, so I tucked the appointment book in the back of my jeans where no one would be able to see it, and then I kept searching. Maybe there was something else recorded there, but I didn't have time to uncover it at the moment.

I finished looking around and realized that I had to go into the bathroom with the body before I ran out of time. I walked in, and it took me a second to realize that I was holding my breath. The air in the room was a bit rancid, there was no doubt about it, but I didn't plan on staying there long. The toiletries had been lined up neatly on the sink, and Abel's clothes for the next day were laid out on a chair beside the vanity.

Nothing looked out of the ordinary there.

That left the body.

I knelt down, holding my candle close to him, and studied the corpse. I didn't check it thoroughly by hand like a coroner or even a cop would have done, but I couldn't see any signs of trauma anywhere on him. That didn't mean that he hadn't been hit from behind, stabbed, or even poisoned, but I didn't see any indications that his death had been anything more than a heart attack.

I started to stand when my foot landed on one of the spilled pills that had been dumped out of the bottle in his hand when he'd hit the floor.

I didn't think much about it until I looked at a few other pills and realized that they were different somehow.

That was when I realized that the one I'd nearly stepped on had an *H* embossed on it, while the one beside it looked pristine. Taking out my hanky, I reached down and flipped the blank pill over, just in case it was printed on one side only.

That side was blank as well.

I looked at the *H* pill again, and then studied the rest of the pills that were scattered across the floor.

Only three pills had the telltale *H*.

The rest, nearly three dozen, were all blank on both sides.

Had someone monkeyed with Abel's medication? If so, what he thought he was taking for his heart might indeed just be some kind of harmless placebo. If they had killed him that way, it would be a slow and random form of murder, waiting for him to take the wrong pill when he needed it most.

But I knew in my heart that it had been murder nonetheless.

I realized that Jake had wanted to preserve the scene, but I needed evidence when I told him what I'd found, so I scooped up one of the *H* pills and one of the blank ones so I could show them to him later.

It was really all that I could do at that point.

I looked around for another few seconds, and then I realized that my time had run out. I couldn't afford for Jasper to catch me exploring Abel's room after we'd made a point of locking both rooms to preserve the scenes for the police.

I made sure the appointment book was still tucked firmly behind my back, and then I stepped back out into the hallway.

After locking the door behind me, I was ready to join them in Beatrice's room when Jasper came out.

The moment he saw me, his gaze narrowed. "Where were you just now, Suzanne?"

It amazed me how easily lying to the man came to me once I suspected him of killing his sister. "I thought I could handle seeing her, but when I started to walk in behind you two, I realized that I couldn't deal with it." I tried to make myself sound weak and scared, which honestly wasn't all that difficult to do, given the circumstances.

"I get it," Jasper said, looking at me with a hint of sympathy. "I still can't believe it happened."

"Well, there's no arguing that it did," Jake said as he closed and locked Beatrice's door behind us. "You understand that we can't keep popping into her room whenever you feel like it," Jake said a bit coolly.

"I said I was sorry, okay?" Jasper told my husband.

"What did I miss?" I asked.

"Jasper decided to rearrange Beatrice's body," Jake said.

"She looked uncomfortable," he whined.

I wanted to tell him that she was long past caring about that when Jake spoke up. "I told you when we went in that you couldn't touch anything. Come on, let's go down and see the others."

Jasper nodded, but not before reaching back and touching Beatrice's door again, as though she could somehow feel his presence through it. It was an odd way to act, and that was saying something, given what we'd all been through recently.

As Jasper walked down the steps, Jake told him, "I need a second with my wife."

I knew that he wanted to confer with me in private about what I'd found, but I needed to give Jasper an excuse to believe that it was for something else. "I'm sorry. I just need a little comfort from my husband, and I don't want to get it in front of everyone else."

"That makes sense," Jasper said as he headed down. Before he got to the bottom of the steps he turned and said, "I'll tell them what's happening."

Great. Now everyone was going to think I was too weak to deal with death, when in reality I had most likely seen more dead bodies than all of them combined, if I didn't include Jake.

"Talk to me," Jake whispered as he hugged me. Whether it was in case someone came up the steps looking for us or to give me actual comfort, I didn't care. It felt good being in his arms again, safe, though I had no real reason to feel threatened at the moment.

"I found Abel's appointment book. He didn't want to force Killian back to work. Vera did, but she was blackmailing him to do things he didn't want to do."

"What's your theory, that he finally balked and she gave him a heart attack in retaliation?" He'd said it skeptically, but I nodded in agreement.

"His pills were scattered on the floor, remember?" I asked.

"He was going after his medicine. Or wasn't he?" Jake asked me.

"Most of them were fake," I told Jake. "Someone wanted him to take a placebo and die from it."

Jake started back up the stairs.

I held him, though. "Where are you going?"

"I've got to grab that appointment book and some of those pills for evidence," he said.

"I've got it covered," I told him.

"You disturbed what could be a crime scene after I told you not to?" Jake asked me levelly.

"I had to make an executive decision, so I made it," I told him, not backing down.

"Good job, Suzanne. I would have done exactly the same thing in your place."

As I handed the key back to him I was about to answer when Killian called out, "Are you two coming back down here, or do we have to come up there?"

"We're coming," Jake said as he took my hand and led me back to the group. I was positive now that we had at least one murderer among us, and maybe even two.

If we all made it through till dawn without someone else dying, it was going to be a miracle, at least as far as I was concerned.

Chapter 17

"WHAT'S GOING ON WITH you two, anyway?" Vera asked us as we rejoined them in front of the fireplace.

Before I replied, I stopped and grabbed another donut, more out of nervous energy than anything else. "What can I say? I wanted a hug from my husband," I said.

She rolled her eyes, but I was determined to let it go.

Killian wasn't, though. "Vera, seeking comfort right now is the most sane thing anyone can do. Don't judge her for it."

"As far as I'm concerned, it's a sign of weakness to need someone else," she said flatly.

"Maybe so," I said, "but if it is, it's a weakness I'm willing to accept about myself."

"I think it shows strength," Killian said, rising to my defense again. "I wish I'd shown my wife and daughter a bit more vulnerability while I still could."

Jake patted his friend's leg. "You've done the best you can."

"Maybe, but my best wasn't good enough," Killian said sadly.

"You might not be able to show your wife that, but there's still time to show your daughter how you feel about her," I said.

"I wish that were true, but I'm afraid it's not," Killian said, his voice breaking.

"Boss, you don't have to tell anyone else what happened," Hank said, stepping up and putting a big hand on the man's shoulder.

"I don't know why I'm hiding it. It doesn't matter anymore. Nothing does," Killian said. "I got the call in my room just before the power and phone line went out.

"Leandra died last night."

"What? Why didn't you tell us?" Jake asked him urgently.

"What good would it have done? She's gone, and I'm all alone. There's nothing left for me anymore."

Jasper said, "You've still got me, Uncle K."

It wasn't much of a consolation prize, as far as I was concerned. But had Jasper known of his cousin's passing by accident somehow? If he had, it might have given him the impetus to clout his sister on the back of the head and chuck her over the balcony. As far as I'd heard, that would make Jasper the sole heir to Killian's fortune now, a motive for murder if ever there was one.

"Thanks," Killian said, his heart clearly not into it.

"You knew about this earlier?" I asked Hank.

"He had to tell someone, and I was nearby at the time," Hank said. "I've known Killian and Leandra from before she even got sick."

"I'm sorry I kept it from all of you," Killian said. "I thought I could keep it all in, but I know now that it was a mistake."

"I'm so sorry for your loss," I told our host. That explained the strain I'd seen in his face, though losing his niece at nearly the same time as he'd lost his daughter might have been too much for a normal man to bear.

"I appreciate it, but I can't talk about her, not just yet." Killian stood and headed up the stairs.

"Where are you going?" Jake asked him.

"I need to be alone. I'm going to the tower," he said.

"I'll come with you, Boss," Hank said as he stood.

"No. I need you to go downstairs and check on the heating system. I'm afraid that battery bank might fail, and then where will we be?"

"Are you sure?" Hank asked, clearly not wanting to be separated from his boss.

"I'm positive," he said.

The handyman started to leave, as did Killian, when Jake said, "I hate to do this, but we all need to stay together until help gets here."

Vera scoffed. "You have no power here. You're an *ex*-lawman, remember? I'm going to bed if anyone needs me, but don't try to get into my room. I may have an aversion to locked doors, but I'll have an unpleasant surprise under my pillow for anyone who decides to come after me."

"Are you honestly armed, Vera?" Killian asked her incredulously.

"Maybe I am, and maybe I'm not, but a girl has the right to protect herself, doesn't she?" she asked her former boss.

"Why *shouldn't* we leave the room?" Jasper asked. I hadn't expected him to be the voice of reason, and it caught me by surprise. "Don't you trust any of us? We haven't given you any reason to act the way you're acting."

"I don't know about that. I can think of a couple right off the top of my head," Jake said with a frown.

"Name one," Vera snapped.

"As a matter of fact, I can name two. Beatrice and Abel," Jake answered. He glanced at me and I nodded my approval of him disclosing what we thought. After all, it might be the only way we could keep everyone together without resorting to him pulling his weapon on them.

"What about them?" Killian asked. "Beatrice killed herself and Abel had another heart attack."

"At least that's what the killer or killers wants the rest of us to think," I said.

"Did you honestly just say *killers*?" Vera asked. "Let me get this straight. Not only do you believe that two murders happened last night, but they might have been committed by two different people? Do you have *any* idea how ridiculous that sounds?"

"Nevertheless, it's true," Jake said, standing.

"Who killed Beatrice?" Jasper asked as he grabbed my husband's shirt as though he was going to attack him.

Jake brushed his grip loose and shoved Jasper backwards onto a chair. "Don't make me do that again," he said as Jasper struggled to stand. "I won't be so gentle next time."

"That was gentle?" Vera asked. "You can try to manhandle me too, but I still think your wife is crazy."

"Maybe she is, but I agree with her," Jake said.

"Surely you aren't making these accusations wildly," Killian said. "At least tell us why you think as you do."

Jake started to shrug when I spoke up.

"You might as well tell them. They have a right to know," I said.

"Yeah, I suppose that's true enough." My husband turned to the others and explained, "Beatrice died from a blow to the back of the head, as far as I can tell."

"Falling twenty or thirty feet will do that to you," Hank replied as he shook his head.

"If she fell, why was she on her back when she landed and not her face?" Jake asked. "You all saw her. There wasn't a blemish on her."

"Couldn't she have flipped over onto her back on the way down?" Vera asked.

"It might be remotely possible, but I don't think that it's very likely," Jake answered. "My guess is that someone hit her from behind, dragged her to the balcony, and then shoved her over the edge."

"Who would be strong enough to do such a thing?" Jasper asked. "I certainly couldn't have done it, and I doubt if Vera could have, either."

"I'm stronger than I look," she protested.

"Let me get this straight. You *want* us to think you might have done it?" I asked her.

"Of course not. The whole thing is crazy. That girl killed herself and we all know it," Vera answered angrily.

"I think someone took advantage of her threats to kill herself in the past to make it look as though she finally went through with it," I said softly.

"I don't know. It sounds kind of sketchy to me," Hank said. "What do you think, Boss?"

"Right now, I don't know what to think," Killian said. "Even if you're right about Beatrice, that doesn't explain how Abel was murdered."

"Somebody switched his heart medication," I said.

"How could you possibly know that?" Jasper asked me.

"I found these up in his room just now," I said as I pulled out my hanky and displayed the pills I'd recovered. "I'm betting that his legit meds have an H on them, but most of the pills scattered on the floor up there were blank on both sides."

"Who would kill someone that way?" Killian asked me, clearly confused by my explanation.

"Someone who thought they had some time for one of the placebos to make it to their place at the head of the line," I answered. "They wanted Abel dead, but they wanted it to look like a random heart attack. The fact that he died around the time Beatrice did was just a coincidence."

"You clearly think that Jasper killed his sister..." Vera said as the man leapt off the chair and went for her throat.

It had caught all of us off guard, except for Hank. To my surprise, he punched Jasper once, knocking him down and out in an instant.

Jake said, "Thanks for stepping in."

"You would have done it yourself if you hadn't been standing over beside your wife," Hank said. He then turned to Killian. "Sorry about that, Boss, but I'd be lying if I said I hadn't wanted to do that since I met the man."

"He *is* a bit of a weasel, isn't he?" Killian asked. "But why would he kill his own sister? He was devoted to her."

"Maybe he wanted to inherit everything from you when you had a 'misfortunate accident' later yourself," Jake said.

"He'd kill Beatrice and then me, just for *money*?" Killian asked as he shook his head.

"Folks have done a lot worse for a great deal less," Jake said.

"Well, when he wakes up, he's going to be in for a surprise," Killian said. He walked over to one of the tables and grabbed a handy pen and sheet of stationery. After writing a few things down, he called Jake and me over. "I need you two to witness this to make it legal."

"What are you doing, writing him out of your will right here and now?" I asked as I glanced at the document.

"It's what I threatened to do yesterday after dinner," Killian admitted. "I don't want another second to go by before I actually do it."

I nodded and took the pen from him. Before I signed my name though, I read it through. "Are you sure about this, Killian?"

"With Leandra gone, it's the only thing that makes any sense at all to me anymore."

I glanced at Jake, who had read it over my shoulder. He just shrugged, so I signed my name and dated it before handing it to Jake.

Jake did the same, and then gave it back to Killian. "There you go."

"Who did you leave your money to, Killian?" Vera asked. "Did you finally decide to do the right thing by me and leave me everything?" The look of greed in her glance was obvious even in the light being thrown off by the fire.

"Sorry. You've gotten the last dime you're going to get out of me," he said.

She looked disgusted. "If I didn't get it, then who did?"

"Hank does," Killian said as he pointed toward his handyman.

Chapter 18

"ME? BOSS, THAT'S CRAZY," Hank said, clearly stunned by the sudden turn of events. "I don't want your money. I want you to live forever." There was no doubt in my mind that the man was completely sincere as he said it.

"As much as I appreciate the sentiment, we both know that's not going to happen," Killian said. "You've stood by me for years, and you should be rewarded for your loyalty."

"I don't know what to say," Hank stammered.

"That's a first then, isn't it?" Killian asked him with a slight grin.

"Wow. Just wow," Hank said as Jasper started to stir. The moment he regained his senses, he said, "You struck me! Uncle K. I demand that you fire that brute!"

"That's going to be kind of hard to do, since I just made him my sole heir," Killian said. "If you want to dispute it, then Hank will see you in court, I'm sure. Jake, Suzanne, and Vera will all testify that I did it of my own free will."

"Of sound mind, I'm not so sure about," Vera said.

"Watch your step," Killian told her.

"You know what? I don't think I will." She turned to Jasper and added, "If you want to fight him in court, I'll back you up that he wasn't thinking straight when he did this. I've got enough money to pay for the best lawyers that money can buy."

Jasper didn't immediately jump on the offer. "What's in it for you? I can't imagine that you're doing it out of the goodness of your heart."

"It's simple enough. After we win, I get half," Vera said.

"That's insane," Jasper replied.

"Think about it. Which would you rather have, all of nothing or half of more than you'll ever be able to spend in your life?" Vera asked him.

"As much as I enjoy hearing you two plot to overturn my will, Jake wasn't finished when Jasper interrupted. I trust that won't happen again," Killian asked his nephew.

Jasper was about to reply when he looked up to see Hank moving closer to him. "I'll be quiet, at least for the moment," he said.

"I'm sure that's the best we can hope for," Killian said. "Go on, Jake. You've got the floor. Did he kill Abel, too?"

"I don't think so," Jake explained. "He didn't have a motive, unless Abel caught him as he was getting rid of Beatrice's body. If that had happened, he wouldn't have been able to plan such an intricate attack that wasn't time sensitive. No, whoever killed Abel has known him for quite a while."

"Well, *I* certainly had no reason to want to see him dead," Killian said.

"I've known him for years myself," Hank said, "but the two of us got along just fine."

"Just say it. I know you're all thinking it," Vera said.

"You had motive, any one of us had the means, but you had the most opportunity," I said, stepping in. "You had a meeting with Abel that didn't go very well recently, did it?"

"Are you talking about that nonsense out on the balcony earlier?" she asked. "So we had an argument. Big deal."

"No, I'm talking about you blackmailing him to get him to take your side against Killian earlier," I said.

"How could you possibly know about that?" Vera snapped.

"I read his appointment book," I said. "Did you realize that he made notes after every meeting he had? It must have just started recently, and I have to wonder if his mind wasn't slipping a little."

"It was," Killian said. "He was in the early stages of Alzheimer's, and he didn't want anyone else to know."

"So *that's* why he fought me about forcing you back into the business," Vera said. "Suddenly it's all starting to make sense."

"If you'd known, would you have still switched his meds on him?" I asked her.

"I didn't kill anybody," Vera insisted.

"So you say," Jasper answered.

"Shut up, killer," she told him.

He started to get up again when Hank got there quicker than I could have imagined. "Stay right where you are, Sparky."

"Why are you calling me that?" Jasper asked.

"They use the electric chair in this state, don't they?" Hank asked.

"Not anymore," Jake said. "Now it's lethal injection."

"I didn't kill anybody!" he shouted, and despite Hank's earlier threat, he started to stand again.

With one hand on his chest, Hank had him back in his seat with a great deal more force than I thought was entirely necessary, not that I blamed him for doing it.

"I didn't do it," Jasper said petulantly.

"So you say," Hank answered. "So what do we do now, lock these two up in one of the rooms downstairs until the cops come tomorrow?"

"You can't do that," Vera snapped as she started to get up herself.

"Just because I've never hit a woman doesn't mean that I won't," Hank warned her. "You need to behave yourself."

"I don't think so," Vera said as she pulled the gun from her robe that had supposedly been upstairs under her pillow. I couldn't believe that Jake and I hadn't searched her the moment we'd heard that she had a weapon, but in our defense, a great deal had happened in a short amount of time.

I just hoped we didn't end up paying for it with our lives.

Chapter 19

"TAKE IT EASY, VERA," Jake said calmly. "There's no need for this."

"You're not locking me up like some kind of animal!" she shouted as she started toward the front door. "You shouldn't have pushed me!"

"I'm sure you had your reasons to do what you did," I said calmly. "After all, Abel threatened you yesterday. Jake and I saw it. There were extenuating circumstances."

"I didn't do it!" she shouted at me, pointing the gun at my heart as she said it. "How many times do I have to tell you that?"

"Give us the gun and we'll discuss it," Killian said as he started to take a step toward her.

"Take one more step and you'll be dead before your goons can get to me," she said as the gun swung back at him. I knew that Killian could act rashly based on what had happened when he'd rushed his daughter's attacker, and I doubted that Jake could draw his weapon fast enough to stop her.

He tried, though.

She was faster than I expected as she swung back on Jake. "If you finish drawing that gun, you're a dead man. I may act sophisticated, but I grew up on a farm, and my daddy made sure I could shoot just about as soon as I could walk."

Jake's hand dropped away, and I let a deep breath out. It was clear from the way Vera handled her weapon that she was no stranger to firearms, and besides, she had a head start on my husband.

Then Vera did something that surprised me.

She pointed her weapon at me again.

"Now do us all a favor and take that gun of yours out nice and easy," Vera said without looking at Jake. "If you try to get a shot off, your wife is dead."

"Jake, do what you have to do," I said firmly. "You have my blessing. No matter what happens, I love you."

I saw him hesitate for a second, and then he did as Vera ordered. "I love you, too," he said as he dropped his gun on the chair.

"Suzanne, pick it up and bring it to me," Vera commanded.

I was two steps away from it when she barked out, "No! I changed my mind. Sit back down. It would be just my luck that he taught you to shoot."

Jake had given me a few lessons, and I had been contemplating taking a run at her just as she'd suspected that I might. Wow, this woman was extremely good at reading people, because she'd just nailed me as though she could hear my thoughts.

"Jasper, grab it with two fingers and bring it here," she said as she looked at the man with scorn.

"I detest guns," Jasper said. "I don't want to touch that thing."

"That's why you're perfect for the job," she said. "Don't try to get heroic either, or you'll be joining your sister upstairs."

Jasper did as he was told, and as he carried the gun toward Vera, he said, "I still don't know why you had to kill her. Did she see you kill Abel or something?"

Vera's face got red, and I saw her hand squeeze the grip tighter. "What do I have to do to convince you people that I didn't kill anybody?"

"You could start by putting that gun down," Jake told her.

"There is no chance of that happening, sport," Vera said. "If I do that, I lose all of the power, and with the five of you against me, I don't stand a chance."

"If you didn't do it, then you don't have anything to worry about," I told her.

"Yeah, how many people in prison believed that line at one point in their lives?"

Vera started for the door when I called out, "You're not going outside, are you? It's treacherous out there."

"Maybe so, but it's safer than being in here with you all." She grabbed Hank's jacket, which happened to be on a hook by the door. "If anybody follows me, they're as good as dead."

A second later Vera slammed the door behind her, and she was gone.

"What should we do?" Jasper asked. "We can't just let her get away."

"Where is she going to go?" Hank asked him. "We're safe enough from her while she's out there and we're in here."

Killian grabbed his coat. "We can't let her just die outside alone. I need to talk some sense into her. I've lost too many people in the last twelve hours, and I'm not going to lose another one."

"Whatever you say, Boss, but if you go, then I'm going with you."

"Sorry, but we need to split up into pairs," Killian said. "You and I know this mountaintop, but the two of them don't. Jake, Suzanne, is that okay with you?"

"I don't like it, but we don't have much choice," Jake answered as he looked at me for my approval.

"It makes sense," I said. "I just wish we weren't going out there unarmed."

"We won't be," Hank said. "Boss, I'm going to get some of our protection out of the safe. Is that okay with you?"

"We don't have much choice, do we?" Killian asked. "I don't want anybody to shoot her unless there's no other way to handle the situation, though. Agreed?"

Everyone nodded, and Hank returned a minute later with two guns. "I'm sorry I don't have one for everybody," he said as he tucked one in his pocket and started to hand the other one to Killian. "Here you go, Boss."

"Give it to Jake," Killian said. "He's better with it than I would be."

"Whatever you say," Hank said as he did as he was told. "Take care of him, even if it means shooting her. Do you understand?" he asked before he would release the weapon into Jake's hands.

"I know what I'm doing," he said, and somehow Jake managed to wrestle the gun from Hank's grip despite him holding onto it tightly. Hank was tough, but he looked it. Jake was also strong, but that could be deceptive, especially compared to the big man.

"Then let's go after her," Hank said after I'd given everyone lit candles.

"Suzanne, stay close to him," Jake told me on our way out.

"Be careful out there," I said.

"Right back at you," he replied with a smile.

"You need a coat, too," Killian told his handyman.

"I've got one I keep on a hook outside by the door. It was wet earlier so I didn't want to mess up the floors in here."

"It's going to be freezing cold to put on," I warned him.

He grinned at me. "I'm a big boy. I reckon I can take it."

"Let's go, then." I'd completely forgotten about Jasper until I started out. "Feel free to come with us," I told him.

"No thank you," Jasper said. "I don't see the point of getting shot trying to save someone who's already killed two people."

"Suit yourself," Jake said. "Why don't you lock the door when we leave? You don't want her circling back on you, do you?"

"I most certainly do not," Jasper said.

Hank waited until Jasper got close to him. "If we have to knock twice, I'm not going to be happy with you. Do we understand each other?"

"We do," Jasper said shakily.

I had a feeling he'd be sitting with his back to the door the second we left. Hank had clearly made an impression on him earlier.

"The fog has gotten worse, hasn't it?" I asked Hank as we headed off in a direction opposite of Killian and Jake.

"Don't worry. I know my way around this mountaintop like the back of my hand," Hank said. "I still don't know why we're all risking our lives to save someone who doesn't deserve it."

"Do you really think she killed Beatrice and Abel?" I asked him as we moved in the eerie calmness of the swirling clouds of white.

"It kind of makes sense in a twisted sort of way," Hank said as he peered into the nothingness. "Like you said, Abel and Vera didn't really get along. Whether she killed Beatrice too or Jasper did it, I couldn't tell you. I hate to say it, but as far as I'm concerned, good riddance. They were both making Killian's life miserable, so I can't say that I'll be shedding a tear for either one of them."

It was a harsh thing to say, and I could hear a hint of anger in his voice that I'd caught a few times before when it came to my fellow guests. "You care a great deal about him, don't you?"

"I'd give my life for him," Hank said.

"It's admirable of you, but why exactly are you so loyal to the man?" I asked him, curious what could inspire that much devotion to someone else.

"It's no real secret. I did something stupid when I was younger, and if it weren't for Killian getting me out of it, I'd still be rotting away in prison," Hank said. "But that's old news."

"Really? I haven't heard the story," I said.

"There's not much to tell. I got a little drunk, and a guy pushed me in a bar. I didn't mean to hit him as hard as I did. The judge was a third cousin of his or something, and he was ready to throw the book at me when Killian stepped in. I was working for him as a bagger at his first grocery store, and we got along pretty good. He paid for a decent lawyer, and with the judge knowing that he was being watched, I got off with serving five years instead of life. When I got out, he gave me my old job back, no questions asked."

"I can see why you'd be loyal to him after that," I said.

"That's more than I can say for the rest of *them*," he said as he took another step forward.

Something in Abel's appointment book clicked just then. "Were you here when Abel came to see Killian earlier in the week?"

"I was around," Hank said a bit invasively.

"Where were you when Killian and Beatrice were arguing last night?" I asked him, the pieces suddenly coming together. Just because I hadn't seen him didn't mean that he hadn't been somewhere nearby taking it all in.

"I was around someplace. After all, I had a lot on my plate with you folks being here," Hank said as he turned to look at me suddenly. I saw a flare of his temper just then, and I realized that beneath that calm and jovial surface he liked to project was still a very angry man.

"Still, you must have heard them. I'm guessing from what you said earlier that you were with Killian when he got the news about his daughter, too." I started lagging back a bit, trying to figure out some kind of way to get away from a man I was beginning to suspect was the real killer after all.

"It nearly killed him, and I'm still not sure that it won't. If one more of those ingrates pushes him even just a little bit more, he's not going to survive it."

"Is that why you killed them, Hank? Were you trying to protect your boss?" I asked him.

"What are you talking about?" Hank asked as he turned again to look at me.

I saw that the gun was now pointing straight at me.

I couldn't stop myself, though. "You heard him fighting with Abel when he was here earlier, something that must have greatly upset both men. I'm betting you saw Abel take a pill for his heart and you decided to kill him before you even knew about Leandra's death. I'm guessing that you said something to Beatrice about backing off too, and she took offense. It doesn't take a great leap of faith to figure out that you hit her and then threw her over the balcony."

"You think you're smart, don't you?" Hank asked me with the anger seething to the top now. "I couldn't let them kill him! I did the world a favor getting rid of them both."

"Was that your plan, to knock us all off one by one?" I asked him, searching for somewhere, anywhere, I could hide, but Hank was too close to me to just dart off into the fog.

"You and Jake were safe enough," he said, "but yeah, Jasper and Vera were going to have 'accidents' of their own. When Killian's grip slipped before, I thought he would take care of that one for me, but your husband had to butt in and save him. Never mind. I'll figure something out before we get off this mountain."

"And one day, you'll be richer than anybody you've ever known," I told him, getting ready to throw my candle down and run despite the poor odds in my favor.

"I didn't do it for the money!" Hank shouted, and I saw him raise the gun a bit to get a shot off at me.

Instead, there was another shot, just about close enough to us for me to feel the wind coming off the bullet.

"Jake!" I shouted.

"As a matter of fact, it's Vera," she said as Hank whirled around to return her fire. "That was your only warning."

I couldn't let Hank shoot her when she'd just tried to save me.

I jumped on his back to try to knock the gun out of his hand, but he threw me off as though I were a rag doll.

I thought I was dead, but then I heard Vera's voice much closer than I even realized.

"Last chance. Drop it, or I shoot," she said.

"Go ahead and try it!" he shouted as he started to pull the trigger.

And then she did what she'd just threatened to do.

Chapter 20

"YOU SHOT ME! ARE YOU crazy?" Hank screamed as he clutched at his left leg.

Vera picked up his gun and handed it to me as calmly as if she were passing the mashed potatoes. "I warned you. Lucky for you I know what I'm doing, or that could have ended badly for you."

"Worse than getting shot?" he cried out.

"Well, there's not a lot worse than getting killed." Vera looked at me and asked, "Are you okay, Suzanne?"

"Thanks to you," I said.

"There's no need for you to thank me. I did it out of self-preservation. I heard him tell you that he was going to make sure that I had an 'accident' of my own. I just wanted to do unto him before he could do unto me. Just because I took care of him doesn't make me a saint."

I was about to answer when Jake rushed up and pointed his gun at Vera. "Drop it. You only get one warning."

"She shot me! Kill her!" Hank shouted. He was like a broken record, and I was learning just to ignore him. What a baby. It wasn't as though I hadn't taken a bullet myself, and besides, I had a hard time mustering any sympathy for a repeat killer.

"Jake, she's okay," I shouted as Vera dropped her gun. "She saved me."

"Again, I was just looking out after my own self-interests. He's the one who killed Abel and Beatrice," she told Killian as he joined us.

"Why? Why did you do it?" Killian asked his handyman, honestly surprised by the news.

"It was all for you, Boss," Hank said.

"Hank, you shouldn't have done it," Killian answered, grossly overstating the obvious, at least as far as I was concerned.

"I just couldn't let them kill you inch by inch," he said. "If I had to do over again, I would do it all the same."

He meant it, too, something that sent chills through me.

Killian was about to reply when Jasper came running up. We were easy enough to find. There was a break in the fog, and then the mist quickly dissipated as though on cue. It was almost as though it had decided to lift at exactly the right moment, and the bright moon suddenly reappeared in the sky.

"What's going on, Jasper? Did the gunshots bring you outside?" Killian asked him.

"No, it's your house," Jasper said as he pointed back to it, now clearly visible as it perched on the mountaintop.

"What about it?"

"It's creaking and rumbling like there's a volcano underneath it," Jasper said. "Something's wrong, Uncle K."

"I don't understand. It's on massive piers dug into the granite," Killian said.

"At least that's what your builder told you he did," Jake said.

A moment later we could all feel the vibrations in the ground below our feet as the mountain estate collapsed in on itself and slid out of our view, no doubt making its way to the bottom of the incline to join the road that had slid down earlier.

"It's gone. I can't believe that it's gone," Killian said as he started to walk toward where his new place used to be.

"Don't do it, Killian," Jake said as he put a hand on his friend's shoulder. "It might not be safe."

"*Nothing's* safe around here, is it?" Killian asked as he started to collapse.

Thankfully, my husband was there to catch him just as we heard rumbling overheard.

Evidently the mountaintop had been the last place for the fog to clear.

Otherwise the helicopter never would have risked flying up there to save us all, just a little too late to do two of our party any good.

Chapter 21

"SO, HOW WAS THE SECOND honeymoon?" Momma asked me an hour after we made it back to April Springs later that day. "You're back early, aren't you? I didn't see Jake's truck in the driveway. What happened—did it break down?"

"No, it's still sitting on a mountaintop waiting for the road to get fixed enough to bring it here," I told her. "Jake is returning the rental his friend Killian got for us, and then we're going shopping."

"Shopping? Really? I try and try to get you to shop and you never want to do it. What's Jake's secret?"

"I lost a bunch of clothes in an avalanche," I told her simply, and then I went about finishing up the dishes I'd been doing when she'd come in.

"Right, and I lost my diamond broach in the monsoon," she said, and then she studied my expression for a moment. "Hang on. You're serious, aren't you?"

"Dead serious," I told her.

"Suzanne Hart, did you somehow manage to get yourself into trouble in one night?"

"I did at that," I said as I finished putting the last dish away.

"Well, pour me a cup of coffee and tell me all about it," Momma said.

"I would, but you wouldn't believe it," I told her as I did as she requested.

"Try me. I've known you your entire life, so nothing you do would surprise me."

"Believe it or not, this time it wasn't my fault," I explained.

"Tell it to someone who will believe it," she answered with a smile.

"I would, but I might have trouble tracking somebody like that down," I answered, happy to be with her again. "How's your world been since I've been gone?"

"Well, now that you ask, that's the reason I came by. Since you turned down my job offer, something I still don't quite understand, I've hired someone to be my assistant."

"Good for you. Is she nice?" I asked, basically just making a bit of polite conversation.

"Nice? I don't know if anyone would describe her that way, but she's efficient, and I can trust her. At least I think I can. I was hoping you'd talk to her and tell me what you think."

"Wow, I'm honored that you trust my judgment that much," I told her.

"No matter how much I tease you, young lady, I have a great deal of respect for your ability to size people up."

"You might want to rethink that once you hear about what happened to us," I said. "I was two feet from a serial killer and didn't have a clue until almost too late what was really going on."

"Honestly, I can never tell if you're being serious or you're just giving your old mother a hard time."

"The truth is I'm not even always entirely sure, but right now it's spot on the money, believe me."

"Then I may need something a bit stronger than coffee to be able to hear this," she said.

"That might not be a bad idea."

As we settled onto the couch, I started to tell her what had happened to Jake and me, trying to downplay the very real dangers we had faced, but failing spectacularly.

After I finished hitting the highlights, she said, "I thought you were going to take a long break from digging into things like this."

"I thought so too, but trouble seems to find me wherever I go," I told her.

Momma patted my arm affectionately. "Well, as long as you don't stray too far away from me, I'm okay with it."

"I love you too, Momma," I told her with a smile.

Jake had had the right idea getting us both a break away, but I knew that without a doubt April Springs was where I belonged, and it would most likely be a long time before I left town again.

Even then, I had a hunch that trouble would still find its way to my doorstep.

And that was okay with me. As long as I was surrounded by the people I loved, I could handle anything that life threw my way.

At least I hoped so.

RECIPES

Cinnamon Cranberry Drop Donuts

I like to play with holiday flavors year-round, but especially around December. There's something about the Yuletide season that gets my baking gears spinning. That's not to say that there aren't times that I'm looking for quick, easy, tasty, and new combinations, though. I know, it's a tall order, but hey, isn't that what having fun in the kitchen is all about? I make this recipe with chocolate chips sometimes, and you should feel free to add a handful if you are so inclined, but there's something simple and elegant about cranberry and cinnamon together, at least in my opinion.

The simple part of this recipe comes from the premade mix I use to enhance the final outcome, but don't tell anybody! It can be our little secret. These drop donuts are great on the go, or sitting by the fire. Give them a try when you're too tired, too stressed, or just too anything to dig out a recipe that contains more than a few steps. Just remember to hide the packet mix bag after you're finished making donuts, and nobody will ever know just how easy these donuts really are to create!

Ingredients

1 packet (7 ounces) prepackaged cinnamon biscuit mix (plain will work, too)

1/2 cup whole or 2% milk

2 tablespoons granulated sugar

1/3 cup dried cranberries (raisins will work as well if you don't care for cranberries)

Optional

2 tablespoons semisweet chocolate chips

Directions

Heat enough canola oil to 360°F to fry your donuts.

In a medium-sized bowl, combine the prepackaged mix, milk, and sugar, stirring until the dry ingredients are incorporated into the wet, but being careful not to overstir the mix.

Next, add the dried cranberries (and chocolate chips if you so desire), mixing them in as well, but again being careful not to work the batter too much. It's better to have a few small lumps than an overworked mix.

Drop bits of dough using a small-sized cookie scoop (the size of your thumb, approximately) into the hot oil. Fry for 3-4 minutes, turning halfway through.

Yields 10-12 donut drops

Ginger and Clove Donut Treats

Lately I've been playing with an air fryer I just bought, and I'm trying to work up some basic recipes for it. This is my first attempt at making one exclusively to be air fried, and to be honest with you, I'm still not quite sure if I've gotten it right yet. That's the thing to remember, though. Even salted old pros have to go through their share of failed attempts when they start something new, and I always like to share my failures as well as my successes with you all. So try this one with a measure of forgiveness in your heart if they don't turn out well for you. If you want to wait until I'm a little more confident in what I offer, feel free to make them and then laugh at me. Trust me, I'll be laughing right along with you. Ginger and Clove? Seriously? What was I thinking?

Ingredients

Wet

2 eggs, beaten

1 cup milk (whole or 2%)

1 stick butter, melted (8 ounces)

1/2 cup brown sugar, dark

2 tablespoons molasses

1 teaspoon vanilla extract

Dry

2 cups flour, unbleached all-purpose

2 teaspoons ground ginger

1 teaspoon ground clove

1 teaspoon cinnamon

1 teaspoon baking soda

1/4 teaspoon nutmeg

1/2 teaspoon salt

Directions

Preheat your air fryer for 320°F, setting the timer for enough time to fry all of your donuts.

While it is preheating, beat the eggs, then mix in the milk, melted butter, brown sugar, molasses, and vanilla extract. In a separate bowl, combine the flour, ginger, clove, cinnamon, baking soda, nutmeg, and salt.

Place the batter in a silicon mold or metal donut pan in your air fryer after coating lightly with some nonstick spray.

Air fry until brown, 8-10 minutes, and start on the next batch.

Yields 10-12 donuts, depending on your mold or pan.

*Note: If you don't have an air fryer, you can still make these in a conventional oven, baking for 7-9 minutes at 350°F, or until brown.

Suzanne's Classic Meatloaf

I have a few basic meatloaf recipes I like to use, but this one is a consistent performer in the kitchen, at least as far as my family is concerned. The combination of beef and pork really makes the meatloaf flavorful and juicy, but if you want to go with straight ground beef, that works out well, too. This started off as a family recipe, but I've enhanced it enough over the years that it's now my own. I suspect those who come after me will add their own tweaks to the recipe, and I couldn't be happier about that. Recipes, at least as far as I'm concerned, should never stop growing and evolving, but don't tell my mother that! She heartily disagrees with me on that point, but hey, what she doesn't know can't hurt her, right?

Ingredients

1 pound ground beef (I like the 80/20 blend for the fat content. This isn't a place to avoid extra calories, at least in my opinion.)

1/2 pound ground pork. (You can use spicy sausage mix if you want to really jazz it up, but it's your call.)

1 chopped onion, medium

1 chopped red bell pepper

½ cup bread crumbs (Italian work fine too)

2 eggs

½ cup catsup

1 teaspoon Worcestershire sauce

Directions

Preheat the oven to 350°F.

In a large bowl, combine the ground beef, ground pork, onion, pepper, bread crumbs, eggs, catsup, and Worcestershire sauce. Mix well. Like Suzanne, I like to use my clean dry hands for this step, since I've never had much luck using any kind of utensil to get the blend I want, but I understand if that's a little too hands-on for you, so feel free to improvise with any handy tool you happen to prefer.

Next, spray a 9X5 loaf pan with nonstick cooking spray and press the mix into the pan. This next step isn't necessary, but I like to coat the top of the meatloaf with catsup so it cooks in while it's baking, but again, that's your decision.

Bake for 65-85 minutes, or until the juices run clear when you pierce the top of the loaf.

Let rest for five minutes before serving.

I'm not about to give you an amount this serves. It depends on the size of your slices, paper-thin, or slab-sized. I'm sure I don't need to tell you all what size I like. The bigger piece the better, in my book.

Light Baked Cake Donuts

These aren't air fried, but they taste light and airy, something that is sometimes hard to accomplish with a donut! My usual recipes seem to be on the dense side, which is all well and good, but these defy that logic. They aren't the easiest donuts in the world to make, and to be honest with you, one member of my family absolutely hates them, but they have their own fans, so they aren't completely out of my lineup, though I always make something extra for the lone dissenter.

Ingredients

Wet

1 egg, beaten

1/2 cup sugar, white granulated

1/2 cup buttermilk

1/8 cup canola oil

1 tablespoon butter, melted

1 teaspoon vanilla extract

Dry

1 cup flour, unbleached all-purpose

1 teaspoon baking powder

1/4 teaspoon nutmeg

1/8 teaspoon salt

Sweet orange marmalade as a topping

Directions

Preheat the oven to 350°F.

In one bowl, beat the egg thoroughly, then add the sugar, buttermilk, canola oil, melted butter, and vanilla extract.

In a separate bowl, sift together the flour, baking powder, nutmeg, and salt.

Add the dry ingredients to the wet, mixing well until you have a smooth consistency.

Using a cookie scoop, drop walnut-sized portions of batter into small muffin tins, silicon molds, or your donut maker, and bake at for 6-10 minutes or until golden brown.

Top with marmalade while the donuts are hot.

Yields 6-10 small donuts

If you enjoy Jessica Beck Mysteries and you would like to be notified when the next book is being released, please visit our website at jessicabeckmysteries.net for valuable information about Jessica's books, and sign up for her new-releases-only mail blast.

Your email address will not be shared, sold, bartered, traded, broadcast, or disclosed in any way. There will be no spam from us, just a friendly reminder when the latest book is being released, and of course, you can drop out at any time.

Other Books by Jessica Beck

The Donut Mysteries
Glazed Murder
Fatally Frosted
Sinister Sprinkles
Evil Éclairs
Tragic Toppings
Killer Crullers
Drop Dead Chocolate
Powdered Peril
Illegally Iced
Deadly Donuts
Assault and Batter
Sweet Suspects
Deep Fried Homicide
Custard Crime
Lemon Larceny
Bad Bites
Old Fashioned Crooks
Dangerous Dough
Troubled Treats
Sugar Coated Sins
Criminal Crumbs
Vanilla Vices
Raspberry Revenge
Fugitive Filling
Devil's Food Defense
Pumpkin Pleas
Floured Felonies
Mixed Malice

Tasty Trials
Baked Books
Cranberry Crimes
Boston Cream Bribes
Cherry Filled Charges
Scary Sweets
Cocoa Crush
Pastry Penalties
Apple Stuffed Alibies
Perjury Proof
Caramel Canvas
Dark Drizzles
Counterfeit Confections
Measured Mayhem
Blended Bribes
Sifted Sentences
Dusted Discoveries
Nasty Knead
Rigged Rising
Donut Despair
Whisked Warnings
Baker's Burden
Battered Bluff
The Classic Diner Mysteries
A Chili Death
A Deadly Beef
A Killer Cake
A Baked Ham
A Bad Egg
A Real Pickle
A Burned Biscuit
The Ghost Cat Cozy Mysteries

Ghost Cat: Midnight Paws
Ghost Cat 2: Bid for Midnight
The Cast Iron Cooking Mysteries
Cast Iron Will
Cast Iron Conviction
Cast Iron Alibi
Cast Iron Motive
Cast Iron Suspicion
Nonfiction
The Donut Mysteries Cookbook